StepPsycho

Tangled hearts, Twisted fates

MaryseMarullo

DEDICATION

To the slutty girls who love masked men, strong women,
action, and big dick.
He's a masked psycho, but at least he's on a path, so,
love that.
xxx

A special thanks to Elizabeth Machkovski who helped
me editing this book.

TO ME.
FUCK THEM ALL. YOU DID IT.

CONTENT WARNING

For adults only/ The content of this book may be triggering and disturbing to some readers. This is a dark romance thriller. Please take a warning that the content is for adults only. This book contains dark subjects, the action involving multiple uses of weapons, and detailed descriptions of several types of violence. If you're uncomfortable with dark romance, don't read this book. It's a dark romance with a killer, psycho, possessive, and morally grey. Touch her, and you'll die, MMC. It's also a forbidden and taboo romance. It's a thriller with a dark plot.

<u>Several sexual and topics aspects of the book can be disturbing for some people. The subjects include the following:</u>

Age gap, Death, Murder
Anal sex, Praise, BDSM, Knife play, CNC
Blood play, Mature language, Dubcon
Child and innocent suffering, Child neglect, Trauma, Gun violence, Kidnapping
Degradation, Mask kink, Nicotine
Emotional Abuse, Possession, Sick behavior
Gore, Psychopath behavior, Violence
Manipulation, Orgasm denial, Suicidal thoughts
Pain, Primal play, Stepbrother/Stepsister

This work's characters, events, and storyline are entirely fictional. Any resemblance to real persons, living or dead, or actual events is purely coincidental. The author has drawn inspiration from various sources, but the primary focus of this book is a challenging and complex subject matter. While the author has endeavored to approach this topic with sensitivity and diligence, it is essential to note that due to limited information, elements of the narrative have been shaped by the author's imagination. This work is a creative endeavor and should be interpreted as such.

PLAYLIST

TOBY MAI - CITIES (FEAT. TWO FEET)

THE MACHINE - REED WONDER AURORA OLIVAS

CHERIIMOYA - LIVING LIFE, IN THE NIGHT

WIZ KHALIFA - SO HIGH

RYAN OAKES - NUMB

DEMXN - BITCH

BERTIEBANZ - FORMALDEHYDE FOOTSTEPS

FILL THE VOID X THE HILLS- (DJ L BEATS)

TWO FEET - GO FUCK YOURSELF

NIGHT LOVELL — POLOZHENIE

BLEED THE WICKED MENACE-IN THE DARK

DUTCH MELROSE — RUNRUNRUN

LOSE FACE- DANIEL DI ANGELO

OBSESSED (FT. LIMI) - ZANDROS

DEMONS — PLAZA

CHILDREN OF THE SKY — IMAGINE DRAGONS

SLIPKNOT — PSYCHOSOCIAL

INFINITY - JAYMES YOUNG

WORK SONG - HOZIER

CHAPTER 1

A SUDDEN SHIFT

FALLON

Being pretty with blonde hair and all might sound like a win but trust me. It doesn't do much for you when you're stuck in the crummiest part of Vancouver, trying to make it back to your beat-up apartment every night.

I left work at midnight, coming from a shady bar where the men's stares made me feel like prey to be devoured all night. Bastards. I swiftly move down the street, hand plunged into my pocket, tightly gripping my folding knife, while the other searches my handbag to ensure my pepper spray is within reach.

This is the outcome when your mother, a woman of stunning beauty yet gold digger and short-sighted, consistently surrenders control of her destiny to affluent, aging, and rich men. Here you are at age twenty-five, unattached, grappling with paternal complexities, scarcely a penny to your name, and your educational pursuits all but abandoned after high school.

Looking back on my past, it dawns on me how fucking fucked up our lives have been. Home after home, none lasting long enough to plant roots or forge lasting friendships. My father, a man whose life ceased before I could grasp an understanding of who he was, died shortly after I came into this world.

When I observe my mother's history with men, I conclude that perhaps his absence is not as significant a loss as one might think. Valentina always told me that my earliest years were spent in California, born there and all, yet my mind holds no memories from that time.

It's peculiar — the absence of recollection — but then again, perhaps it's a mercy, given the succession of opulent houses and influential weird men who came into our lives, only to view me, I suspect, as nothing more than an inconvenient byproduct of their liaisons with my mother.

I'm entangled in a complex relationship with the male gender, repelled by the memories of those who never saw my worth, even as I feel an unsettling compulsion to seek their approval and affection. I head to our apartment, weaving through the hallway I know like the back of my hand. I find the stairs and hustle up to our floor. As soon as I stepped in, there's my mom sitting at the kitchen table, looking all kinds of happy.

She jumps up and comes at me with a big hug. I should've known. This kind of affectionate gesture always pops up when she has a new boyfriend. "Why do you love me all of a sudden, Mom?" I question with a hint of reluctance, sensing her arm encircling me.

I conjure up a smile that doesn't quite reach my eyes, tinged with an undercurrent of discomfort and distaste. "Quit scowling like that. You'll end up with lines on your face. You're probably curious about my frequent absences over the past month, aren't you?"

Actually, I hadn't spared much thought to it. I've been aware of her trips that stretch to weeks at a time for over a year now. It doesn't bother me; in fact, there's a certain tranquility to my routine when she's away. I can focus, work, save money, and daydream about the day I'll find a purpose.

"So, I'm going to tell you," She starts, raising her left hand so I can see it clearly. My eyes go to her ring. It's a big, fancy gold ring with a large, shiny diamond right in the middle. "Wow. Another husband," I say to her, giving her a half-hearted congratulations. I'm not excited. It's not new.

My bag falls to the ground with a heavy sound as I head to our small, rat-filled kitchen for a bottle of water from the fridge. "He's amazing, Fallon, really! He's got a lot of money. He looks good, tall, and has lots of power."

I nod without really listening. I've gotten used to her talking about the men in her life like they're some gods. I cut her off while she's still chatting away. "Where, Mom?" She stops talking and sits back down.

"What do you mean?"

"Where are you moving now?"

She looks away, and I start paying more attention. She's acting weird. "Fallon. You're coming with me."

"No way. I'm not going with you anymore. I'm twenty-five, Mom. I'm staying here. I'll take care of myself just fine."

"I know you hardly have any money left after paying the bills." She said with a raised eyebrow.

"It helps me stay thin." I force a playful smile on my lips.

"Fallon. He wants to meet you. And I mean it, he's different. He wants us to stay with him for good. He loves me. With him, you could have everything you've ever wanted."

And that's when it hits me, looking into her eyes. She's buying her spiel. Like, seriously, but at the same time, what's holding me back? I've got no one, no friends, no lover down here. Always focus on only surviving.

"Where? " I ask.

"Cali baby! "

I'm packing, and the truth is, I don't have that much to pack: an assortment of clothes, a few books, photographs, my laptop, and my toiletries. Nothing too extravagant. I've always felt the need to keep my possessions to the bare necessities.

I can recall a period in my childhood, around the age of nine or ten, when one of my stepfathers developed an unsettling practice of stroking my thigh over and over during our shared movie nights.

His daughter, slightly younger than me, had quietly shared her relief with me one night. Completely surprised, I asked her, "What's going on?" Then she told me the truth: her dad had been watching me since I arrived.

I was more what he sought, it seems. He left her alone. Feeling really disgusted, I'd told my mom everything, and she was quick to react, "Pack your things. We're leaving tonight."

That evening, she stormed into my room, only to confront the sight of my packed suitcase. Her reprimand came swiftly and sharply. Her scolding was quick and harsh, a sharp slap with a whispered warning telling me off for not being careful enough.

She drummed into me the importance of being sly and discreet. That an abrupt and noticeable exit with excess luggage was impractical and unwise. The sting of the lesson lingered, embedding itself deeply within my consciousness.

From that day forward, I made it a point to avoid becoming too comfortable or established in any place and never fully unpack or root myself in my surroundings.

Sometimes, I wonder what kind of mom Valentina Di Genova is. She could be better. I know that much. But I can't help feeling that deep down, she does love me, even with everything that's happened. Then again, maybe I'm just fooling myself.

I was dead set on keeping my distance from her and moving out soon. But my mom's got this talent for getting people to flip their script. So, it got to me when she started going on about the rich life and her new boyfriend's power.

So, here's the plan: I'm gonna play the part of the perfect daughter, right? Become the apple of his eye. If I pull it off with a bit of style, the guy will probably spoil me rotten without even knowing it.

And that's the game plan till everything hits the fan. Until he grows weary of my mother and decides to show her the door, that's when history will repeat itself, but I'll be off alone and with cash this time. I was amazed when we finally got to the airport, and a lady was there to guide us to our flight. I was expecting the usual crowd of commercial planes. But to my surprise, she escorted us to a door that seems to go outside. "Excuse me, where are you taking us?"

She looks at me from head to toe as if I was the dumbest person for not understanding. But no, I don't get what's happening. "Your flight, ma'am."

Ma'am? What the heck? My mom nudges me, and I look at her. "Franco must have spoiled us by sending his pilot with the jet." THE WHAT?

"Why do you look so shocked? I told you he was wealthy." Beaming with pride, she swells confidently, striding swiftly to keep pace with the woman leading the way. She strolls like she's got every right to own the place, not missing a beat.

I fiddle with my backpack straps, trying to get the darn thing to sit right without killing my shoulders. When the door opens, we step outside, and holy cow, there's this massive, shiny private jet, looking all kinds of fancy. Written in large letters on it, Betto's Enterprise.

Wow, I can't believe my eyes. The plane's shiny white metal is bright in the sun, and its wings seem to twinkle. There's fancy stairs leading up to it, with a posh black carpet that looks super soft and fancy. It's such a flashy show-off move, something only really rich people would do. I'm blown away by how over-the-top it is.

I hurry to catch up with my mom, reaching her as we climb the stairs to get on the plane. Right when we got in, a server came up to us with glasses of a fizzy, yellow drink, fucking mimosa. I take one, still amazed by all the fancy stuff around us.

"Yes, I knew you said he had a lot of money. But this," I said, waving my glass around to point out all the things around us, "this is just way over the top." My tone is one of surprise. She laughed happily and sit down on a big, comfy-looking bench, raising her glass. "Here's to the fanciest life we're about to have."

She sounds hopeful and happy, which is different

from the tough times we had before. We both take a sip from our glasses, and the sound of them clicking together is like starting an amazing new chapter. "Yeah, okay, to that."

CHAPTER 2

THE CASTLE AND ITS ASSHOLES

FALLON

As the aircraft ascended, I resolved to utilize the flight time to research Betto's Enterprise. However, my focus quickly dissolved, overtaken by the novelty of the flying experience. My attention flitted from the flickering entertainment screens to the attentive flight crew weaving through the aisles. Their smiles are practiced yet reassuring.

I caught myself marveling at the elegance of the glassware, each piece reflecting the cabin lights with an opulent gleam. Even the supple leather of the seats demanded my awareness, cradling me in unfamiliar but welcome comfort. The myriad of distractions eclipsed my initial intent, leaving the investigation momentarily forgotten in the altitude-hushed cabin. I'll figure it all out pretty quickly, huh?

Our travels have finally come to an end. We arrived at our final stop much quicker than anticipated, landing at the airport in Santa Clara County. Flying solo on a big plane has its perks. Stepping off the plane, I am immediately struck by the delightful weather and a refreshing, lively aroma that fills the air, quite different from the familiar atmosphere we left behind in Vancouver.

Ever since I turned six years old, Canada has been our home. My mother often told me that staying in the United

States became too painful after we lost my dad, and the memories especially haunted her here in California. Seems like the cash made her totally blank out on that part.

After my father's passing, she remained alone for a considerable period. Back then, she was all about trying to make sure I had what I needed while navigating the waters of grief. That's what she says.

But we were so broke she had no choice but to take this sketchy place crawling with mold. That nasty stuff messed with my lungs big time and landed me in the hospital when I was just a little kid, only five years old.

Once my health was restored, we relocated to the residence of her latest partner, situated within the Canadian borders. It was so new. I only got the memo about him when we were quitting the hospital.

Thinking about this leads me to absentmindedly touch my chest, right where a surgical scar marks the spot that saved my existence.

Valentina once told me that doctors had to meticulously clear out my lungs to pull me back from the brink. I guess I hit the jackpot with a decent rack; as soon as I pop on a bra, my boobs blend and hide that weird scar like magic. My mother glances at me and comes towards me. "Are you okay, sweetheart?"

"First, stop calling me that, Valentina." As we disembark from the aircraft, a man greets us.

He's in a crisp suit, dark sunglasses shielding his eyes, and his head—completely shaven—bears an intricate tattoo, making him scary to be around. "Welcome, Mrs. and Miss Di Genova. My name is Daniel."

He shakes my mother's hand gently, then turns to me. "I am your driver and personal bodyguard." My mom bursts into laughter, acting like a child as she hides behind her hand, sending me an enormous, beaming smile.

"This is so cool!" The thought of having a man in his fifties constantly trailing behind me, acting as my chauffeur and personal shadow, is unsettling. Not cool.

There has to be some method to dissuade him from this duty without causing too much fuss. I'll need to think about that.

Daniel lent a helping hand, guiding us into the enormous truck, its glossy black finish complementing the ultra-dark tint on the windows. I can't help but wonder about the legality of such heavy tinting. But then again, Valentina did say her Franco's a big deal, so maybe he's got the kind of influence that puts him beyond the law's reach.

As soon as our bags are tucked away in the trunk, Daniel hops into the driver's seat. "Alright, ladies, fingers crossed for some luck and lame traffic. We should hit the estate in, like, fifteen minutes tops." And off we go, with the engine purring to life. I have to give it to the guy. He's got his act together. For someone who's probably been around the block, he's got that seasoned pro vibe—or should I say, seasoned pro look, with his slick tie and all.

The Betto manor looms before us, grandeur seeping from its very stones—a testament to the wealth that built it. A wrought-iron gate standing sentinel greets us; its intricate spirals and curls a preface to the opulence beyond.

Valentina checks her reflection in a compact mirror, a last-minute primp, before we enter this new world. The path to the front door is a cobblestone mosaic, each stone likely handpicked for perfection. I can't help but gape at the extravagance that embraces us, the manicured lawns stretching out like green seas dotted with flowerbed islands.

The estate is breathtaking. Yet, despite its splendor, a sense of unease grips me. An ominous energy lingers in the air, sending an involuntary shiver cascading down my spine.

The car stops, and I look around. There are many fancy cars; one in particular, dark gray, catches my eye. I know nothing about cars. But this one seems like it's from a different time. Employees in nice clothes walk around us, opening the car doors for Valentina and me, and I get out to come face to face with a big fountain right in front of the stairs that go up to the house. If I can even call it that. It's more like a castle.

We're ushered in by a butler whose stoic expression manages to convey a welcome without a single word. The air smells faintly of lemon and beeswax—clean and rich. Inside, the manor unfolds like a scene from an old Hollywood movie: marble floors, crystal chandeliers, and a staircase that curves upward, begging for a glamorous descent. It is silent except for the soft echo of our footsteps and the distant sound of a piano playing a classical melody.

The sound waves through the air, a haunting reminder that life here moves to a different beat. Now entirely in her element, Valentina glides across the floor with the grace of a queen claiming her throne. I trail behind, absorbing every detail. The marble beneath my feet is polished and authentic—a stark contrast to the life of fake promises I've left behind. Each breath I take is heavy with a fragrance of power and intimidation.

As we pass a grand mirror, I catch the reflection of myself, a stark anomaly in this world of curated beauty. My ashy blonde hair is a messy crown, and my clean clothes feel suddenly out of place. But there's no time to dwell; the butler opens a set of doors, and we're welcomed into the snake's den. I brace myself, my mother's hand lightly resting on my back, a rare touch that pushes me forward.

We step into the heart of the Betto empire, my pulse racing as the doors close with a soft but final click behind us. What unfathomable secrets does this manor guard? And at what cost will they come to light? As we approach what appears to be a living room with beautiful leather armchairs, there stands the man who is clearly Franco Betto. His presence is a force, the air seeming to thrum with his power. He greets Valentina with a kiss on the cheek that lingers just a moment too long, then turns his attention to me with a gaze piercing my defenses. I can't help but meet his eyes, feeling like a mouse caught in a trap. "Fallon, so lovely to finally meet you," he says, his voice smooth as silk yet edged with a blade. His aura is a tightly woven tapestry of luxury and menace, the ultimate contrast to my chaotic vibrancy.

"Pleased to meet you too, Dad." I smile, thinking my joke is pretty funny. My mom gasps and puts a hand over her mouth. Franco looks at me with no expression. "I see we have another comedian now."

I'm confused. Another comedian? "Just call me Franco. That will be enough, Fallon." He looks at his watch before saying in a voice that breaks his perfect front. "Late again." I almost jumped out of my skin when the doors suddenly swung open and hit against each side's walls. The air around us bristles with his entry, a current that jolts me to the core. He bursts into the room like a savage storm, his presence a raw, untamed force that somehow magnifies my own wild nature. His eyes, a fierce blue, flicker with a spark of recognition - or is it challenge? - as they meet mine.

He's a danger, chaos, and a hint of something more. "Hello everyone." His voice resonates with a deep timbre that vibrates through me, stirring something within.

My eyes move from the tall, mysterious,

handsome man to Franco. His jaw looks clenched, and I notice his fists are so tight that his knuckles are white. Strange. "You're late," Franco says, placing a hand on the shoulder of the other man and walking away with him to talk about something we clearly can't hear, seeing how he whispers. Valentina comes to my side and pulls me out of my staring state. "He is incredibly rude, dangerous, and thoroughly sociopathic. You've gotta stay away from that guy." Before I can curse her for acting like she cares, the men return to us. "Fallon, this is Camden. He's my son." Camden, I walk up to him to shake his hand. He suddenly grabs it and pulls me in, and I bump into him. "It's not a pleasure to meet you, bunny," he whispers in my ear, and Franco coughs to clear his throat, bringing us each back to our place. What the hell? What's his problem? If he thinks he's scaring me, he's wrong.

CHAPTER 3

SOUTH WINGS

FALLON

I trail behind, a quiet storm brewing in my head as the employee guides me through the maze of corridors. What's wrong with Camden? The coward has just been so mean to me for no reason. His swift exit lingers like a phantom touch. The fucker left as quickly as he came, leaving everyone except Franco shocked. Franco immediately told us that we would hardly ever see him. Apparently, the mansion is split in two, with the south wing belonging to Camden. So yeah, I'm like relieved. I seriously can't deal with seeing him again after that crazy meeting earlier. If he believes he can call me Bunny, and I won't clap back... No way, Jose.

This place's a fortress. I tread on carpets that hush my footsteps, passing doors that I imagine hide worlds within worlds. The scent of antique wood mixed with a faint floral aroma envelops me.

I'm led up a small set of stairs, my hand gliding over the smooth walls. The echoes of my heartbeats are like drums in the chamber of my chest—irregular and frantic.

We stop before an imposing door. The employee pauses, an expectant look on her face. The door opens with a gentle creak, revealing an opulent and relaxed space, touched by the sun yet somehow devoid of warmth.

My new room is vast, the furnishings exquisite, the bed an island amidst the sea of extravagance. The fabrics are soft and inviting to the touch, but they feel foreign under my fingertips, like the caress of a stranger.

I'm suddenly aware of the silence, a stark contrast to the lyrical chaos of the life I had in a crappy apartment.

"You have a big closet on the left, and the door on the right is your bathroom, Miss Di Genova."

"Please, call me Fallon." We are almost the same age. It makes me uncomfortable when she calls me miss. "If you allow me, Fallon."

I give her a genuine smile before tossing my bag on the bed when her gentle voice speaks to me again. "Miss Fallon, I must warn you. Just down the hallway here," I walk to the door and look at the hallway. She points with her tiny finger. Barely three meters from my door is another door.

"This door is the division with the mansion's south wing." "You are not allowed to open this door." I give her a thumbs up and say goodbye.

Shadows stick to the walls of my new room. My fingers touch the silk curtains. The material feels expensive. I run my fingers over the interesting old things in my room—items from lives I've never had, stories I've never heard. They stand like silent judges, watching me try to understand this unknown world I've found myself in.

My mind fights against the quiet, a storm growing inside me. I need a fight, voices, something to set off the unease I feel. The thought of Camden, with his mean look, black tattoos, and deep blue eyes, comes to mind, my unexpected enemy. Pushing everything aside, I decide to go explore my new bathroom and turn on the faucet. The bath is large, standing, and sloppy to me. After all, you always feel better and rest after a good hot bath session.

The light dimmed, bubbles surrounding me, I'm enjoying the moment. I can't remember when I took the time to soak. I grab my phone and decide to look up some info on my new stepbrother. I type his name into the search engine and scroll but find nothing. Interesting, it's as though he doesn't exist. Next, I type in Franco's name. A bunch of articles and images pop up. I read each one. They praise the achievements of this fantastic businessman who has risen to the top of high society by himself. Wow, he owns almost all of the country's casinos, many bars and clubs, and restaurants, and he's the founder of the Betto Health Collective Foundation.

I click on the article that goes into detail about the foundation. Okay, maybe he's better than I thought. He gives thousands of dollars every year so that sick children in poverty worldwide can get free healthcare. That's fucking awesome. I put my phone down on the tub's edge and think about my choice to come here. Mom was right. Becoming part of the family will be the best for me and my future if I'm able to tame my new brother. If I'm lucky, I won't see him except during the holidays.

With all the money Franco has, I'll finally live a life of luxury. But I have to watch Valentina, though, to make sure she doesn't act crazy and make Franco leave her. He's my golden ticket.

Fresh, invigorated, and ready to continue this strange day, I quickly get dressed and join Franco and Valentina for the meal.

I walk without paying attention, contemplating the walls with paintings and portraits. When I run into something hard. I look up and see Camden. We stand facing each other like an invisible battlefield between us. "Oh, good. The little bunny," he says in a low, mean voice.

I face him bravely, anger burning inside me. "You can't boss me around, Camden. You don't even know me," I say boldly.

Our standoff begins—a tug-of-war of wills. The air is full of our dislike for each other, a storm held within the big house's walls. "Stay away from me. Stay away from here. Go back to rotting where you came from. You don't belong in a place like this."

Neither of us backs down. We face each other. I can feel fear trying to shake me, but the thrill of the forbidden keeps me standing strong. "I'll not go anywhere." And my heart stops. He smiled. The most beautiful smile I've ever seen. Dimples. Fuck me. "Give me one good reason to let you walk away right now. " My brows knitted together in frustration. "I'm hungry."

Without looking back, I bump his body past it with my shoulder and continue walking. Am I going on the right side? Another idea. As I navigate the sprawling hallways of the Betto mansion, trying to find the damned dining room in this labyrinth of a house, the surveillance cameras perched in every corner catch my wary gaze. They're an eerie testament to the wealth and power at play, a necessary precaution, in a home that's more fortress than residence. It should be comforting, I think, the security—but it's not.

The cameras add to the discomfort coiling in my gut, a presence as tangible as the lens glinting in the obscure lighting. I force thoughts of surveillance from my mind; logically, it makes sense for it to be here. He's powerful and wealthy—it's expected.

But that doesn't reduce the creeping sense of darkness exuding from the walls since we arrived this morning. It feels like I'm being watched, not just by the unblinking eyes of technology but by the mansion itself, whispering tales of things best left unseen.

I round another corner; the silence is oppressive, the distant clink of cutlery against China the only sign that I'm getting closer.

Finally, I found what I was looking for a grand space awash with golden light and the scent of a sumptuous meal, hinting at a warmth that feels absent from the atmosphere. As aromas assail my senses, the shadows cast by the flickering candles do little to dispel the heaviness in the air. I pause at the threshold, gathering my resolve like a cloak around my shoulders. I steady my breathing, preparing to step into my chair, trying to ignore the lingering sensation of darkness clinging to my skin like a second skin. "Hello everyone." My voice is quiet and awkward. I don't like doing this. But I need to get on Franco's good side. He has to like me. He has to see me as a daughter, not just as a product of his new wife's past. "Hello, Fallon. You look lovely." Franco tells me with a smile.

He's a handsome man. He looks in his mid-fifties, with a clean-cut beard, deep brown eyes, and a body that could make twenty-year-olds jealous. "Thank you. I chose the pants and shirt from the wardrobe. Thanks so much for getting clothes ready for me."

I was surprised when, after my bath, the young woman came back to knock on my bedroom door—telling me the time for the dinner and that my wardrobe had been set up for our arrival: clothes, shoes, bags, beauty products, makeup, and jewelry.

"It's my pleasure. I like to spoil my girls." Valentina laughs at his comment and touches his hand on the table. He kisses it, his eyes wide and shocked, staring behind me.

I turn around, and there he is, even taller and more muscular than Franco, his damn blue eyes locking onto me. His scruffy beard barely hides a mean smile. "Hello, sister. Father, Valentina. I'll join you for the meal today." He walks over confidently to a chair next to me and slumps down.

My heart suddenly starts beating faster, and my mom is the first to respond. "I'm happy to hear that. We'll get to know each other better." My gaze shifts between her and Franco, who looks mad to see his son sitting at the same table as us. "Oh, Valentina, I already know you," Camden says. And my eyes land back on him. Unbearable.

He's already eating his salad, and I can't stop my eyes from lingering a bit too long on his manly features that are worthy of a god. He truly is a work of art. His beard, not too long but still present, seems rough and soft at the same time. Almost as dark as his hair.

The diner progressed without a hitch, absent of any peculiar remarks or genuine signs of affection. We engaged in light conversation; I expressed my respect for the charitable work done by Franco's foundation, and he casually mentioned that my chauffeur, Daniel, would be providing me with a guided tour of the city the following morning. He says he asked him to show me places he presumed would pique my interest.

I kept my thoughts to myself, resisting the urge to point out that he couldn't predict my preferences. I settled into my role. Camden's laugh broke through the formality, a rich, resonant sound that strangely stirred a flutter within my abdomen. "Do you have something to say?" I face him, and he puts his hands behind his neck, looking at me with confidence and hate. "Bunny, I don't plan on talking to you." This mother fucker. He gets up and heads for the exit, leaving us again confused.

CHAPTER 4

RUN BUNNY RUN

FALLON

The mansion's corridors seem to stretch into eternity, the carpet swallowing the sound of my footsteps as if erasing my path as I go. I can feel the weight of Camden's earlier presence like a heavy cloak around my shoulders, the silence oppressive, amplifying the isolation in this grand mausoleum of a home.

I refused the help of my butler, too unnerved by the prospect of someone lurking silently at my elbow—a shadowy reminder of the unfamiliarity between myself and this gilded cage. Now I'm fucking lost.

The light fixtures cast a feeble glow, throwing ghastly silhouettes that danced mockingly alongside me. I continue, muscles tensing with the desire to turn and confront whatever phantom stalks my steps, but there's nothing—only the whispering silence and the soft echo of my breathing.

Finally, the door to my bedroom looms before me. With a shaky hand, I push it open. Something isn't right. The room is awash in the pale moonlight that filters through the sheers, turning everything into a spectral version of luxury.

Stepping inside, I'm hit with a wave of foreboding, the air feeling cooler, heavy with expectation. My eyes slowly adjust to the soft light, and that's when I see it—a grotesque offering before me.

There, on the polished floor just at the foot of my grand king-sized bed, is a dreadful sight—a dead rabbit, its fur matted with dark, congealing blood, a violent rupture in the serenity of my sanctuary.

I stand there, petrified, my breath hitching in my throat, chest tight with fear. The acrid scent of death assaults my nostrils, and I feel a visceral urge to retch. The violation of my room with such a brutal symbol sends an icy dread coursing through my veins. But above all, it puts me in a terrible mood. What game is this? A warning? a threat? or some twisted welcome gift?

My mind races with dark possibilities, each more sinister than the last. This isn't just a dead animal; it's a declaration, a sign that the safety I sought within these walls is nothing more than an illusion—a cruel joke at my expense.

I come closer and find a piece of paper attached with a little red ribbon around the animal's neck. I take it and can read:　　　　　Run, bunny.

The moon outside casts a geometric pattern of shadows on the floor, a chilling reminder of the bars of a prison. I realize, with cold certainty, that I may have escaped the shitty streets of Vancouver, but I've waltzed right into a trap far more dangerous and incomprehensible than any back alley.

I force myself to step back, my mind screaming to run and get out. The dead rabbit's unmoving eyes seem to bore into me, a silent witness to the night's grim revelation. I know who it is. It's so apparent, and he knows it. You want to play, brother, I'll fucking play.

The mansion's south wing is shrouded in silence, amplifying every heartbeat in my chest. With the weight of the bloodied rabbit dangling from my grip, I navigate the labyrinthine hallways. My resolve is a flame flickering in me. Adorn with dark portraits and heavy tapestries. The walls watch over my intrusion with silent judgment.

I find him, a vision of raw power and force, battering a box mannequin with focused brutality. Sweat glistens on the landscape of his bare back, each muscle outlined with the precision of a sculptor's chisel.

I stand transfixed momentarily, taking in his sight—this stunning, maddening enigma of a man. "He's so handsome but a complete psycho," I think to myself, my breath catching in my throat.

Fueled by anger and the need for confrontation, I launch the dead animal right at him, the sound of its impact against his skin echoing through the room. He whips around, his expression transforming into one of unadulterated fury.

With speed that belies his size, he is upon me, his hand at my throat, fingers pressing with an intent that drives the air from my lungs. "Why are you here? You shouldn't be!" His snarl is a dangerous rumble in the confined space. I'm troubled to see that receiving a shell makes him react less than seeing me in the forbidden part of the manor.

Unfazed by his grip, I stand my ground. Staring into his storm-tossed blue eyes, I spit back venomously, "Go fuck yourself, Camden." The taste of my defiance is sharp on my tongue. "You owe me some goddamn explanations about this rabbit."

His grip tightens ever so slightly, a predator

assessing its prey, and for a moment, the world narrows down to the heat of his breath and the iron strength of his fingers. But fear of man is a stranger to me, and I refuse to let it take hold.

All these years of being an object, abused, used. All her years of being alone. All these years of defending myself against them and proving that I am somebody. Now I'm numb. I will not cower before this man, this stepbrother, whose anger is as palpable as the tension between us.

Our eyes remain locked in a standoff. Our silence is electric, charged with unspoken challenges and dark promises. He searches my face for a hint of dread but finds none. I am Fallon Di Genova. I will not break.

He lets me go, steps back, and smiles. "Oh, Bunny, you're in a real mess."

"So are you. Explanation for the rabbit?" His grin radiates a warmth that momentarily steals my breath away. "Do the shit for fun little sis. What age are you anyway? twelve." He appears to be a few years my senior, although I suspect he'd withhold that information considering the less-than-amicable rapport we've shared thus far. "You should run." His eyes darken.

"From you?" He closes the distance with me a little bit more. "Maybe, sister. Now, little bunny, this is the last time I'll repeat myself." He tilts his face in my direction and stretches his hand behind me to retrieve an item from the table, his motion closing the distance between us.

As a result, his inked chest is mere inches from my gaze. Prominently displayed is an enormous serpent, inked with such lifelike detail it appears to undulate across his skin, dominating the canvas of his upper body.

When he stands up in front of me, easily a foot taller, he's holding a gun in his hands. "Get out of my fucking wing." His glare bores into me, both chilling and thrilling in its intensity. "Get out," he commands, the gun in his hand not wavering an inch, pointing at my chest.

I should be scared; I know I should be, but instead, a curious calm settle over me. Maybe it's how he fixes me with such focus or how the corners of his mouth twitch with a hidden fury. Whatever it is, I don't back down.

Lifting the barrel of the gun, I place it between my lips, tasting the cold metal, staring defiantly into his eyes. This is a challenge, big bro. I double down on the danger, a reckless grin pulling at my lips.

The world narrows down to this moment, to the silent conversation between predator and prey. Except, in this wordless exchange, Camden isn't sure which role I'm playing. And neither am I.

With a flick of my middle finger, I salute and flip him off with all the sass and lousy attitude I can muster. The tension between us is a living thing, but I won't let it choke me.

I throw his own words back at him, a punchy farewell laced with venom and a hint of something more. "Fuck you," I say, the edges of my vision tinged with the vibrant colors of my rising bravado. "And by the way, I'm twenty-five." I twirl on my heels, my exit marked by the confident bounce of my ass. The sound of my footsteps rings out, a rhythmic beat against the hard floor, the echo of a woman who faces the devil and doesn't blink.

As I leave his wing, the adrenaline sings in my blood, a firework of triumph and defiance. I've stared into the abyss, flirted with the edge, and walked away unscathed.

The night envelops the mansion in a cloak of unsettling whispers, each creaking a foreign language to my ears. I lie awake, a lone island adrift in a sea of luxurious sheets, the events of the evening replaying in the theater of my mind. Camden haunts the edges of my consciousness with his piercing gaze and imposing presence.

My skin still remembers the pressure of his fingers around my throat, the intrusive heat of his body so close to mine, the cold metal between my teeth. My heart aches to rebel, to challenge the tension between us.

I walked away from him, leaving the crimson-soaked bunny for him to clean. It's his problem to tackle. I'm at a loss to comprehend his actions, which feel totally disconnected from real life.

I toyed with the idea of running to Valentina and Franco and telling them about the whole event. But for some reason, even I can't figure out, I refrained from doing so. I have an unsettling feeling, a sense that something is amiss.

There's an itch, stirring deep that I'm compelled to satiate, my hand wandering beneath the sheets in pursuit of relief. The darkness is my only witness as my mind wanders back to him. The imagery of his hands, strong and assertive, ignites a fire within me, a burning desire that cries out for attention.

I am sick. I'm burning up. The temperature is climbing to intolerable levels. In a swift motion, I shove the blankets away, revealing my skin to the room's chilly atmosphere. The abrupt encounter of the cold air against my overheated skin triggers a cascade of shivers along my back, each bump rising in sharp relief. Panting softly, the sensation of my digits brushing against my skin fails to satisfy the yearning for the one who fucking stalks my mind with his muscular presence. The image of the gun he holds flickers through my mind, the way he looked at me with surprise, mingling danger with desire—a risky combination that only fuels my eagerness to tread the fine line between them.

Ugh, he's my stepbrother, and the fact that it's not okay is making me a lot more wet. As desire coils tightly within me, I teeter on the edge of abandon. I'm driven by a hunger that's impossible to deny, my hands moving with an urgency that only deepens my longing. The room's stillness amplifies every sensation, and as I give in to the searing images of Camden's powerful form. As the heat within me builds to an unbearable pitch, I'm overtaken by a shuddering climax that wracks my frame, my cries too loud in the quiet night. And yet, I'm unable to stop, the agony of the pleasure driving me to the brink of recklessness until suddenly, I'm wiped out.

CHAPTER 5

THAI

CAMDEN

The sun's barely up, and already I'm awake, a fucking habit I can't shake off. Without thinking, I head for the shower, letting the scalding water hit me hard, but it does jack shit to scrub away the shitshow from last night.

Steam fills the space, and my mind's dragging me back to that moment that fucking girl comes in there. A fucking demon in the night. My uninvited guest—storming into my zone, bold as hell, messing with my head. My little bunny had no right to be there, but she just waltzed in. She had the guts to challenge me, something no one's got the balls to do. Damn, she's got nerve. It's a rare fucking thing—nerve.

My world? It's full of spineless cowards. But Fallon? She's a fucking wildfire, chucking that bloody carcass at me like she's throwing down the gauntlet. Her honey-colored eyes burned in mine. I had my finger on the trigger. Ballsy move considering I could have killed her on the spot.

The water's hammering down, but it's her fucking defiance that's crawling under my skin. She's stuck in my head, and I can't shake her out. I got this image of her, with the steam clinging to her, and I can't help but crack a wicked grin.

I want her to be mine, my little bunny. But I can't do that to her right now. She has to go. And one day, I would chase her, keep her forever. Except Fallon might hold her fucking ground. She's the kind of fire that could burn me if I let it.

I've seen all sorts, but she's a different breed and doesn't seem to give two shits about fearing me, and that alone gets me going.

I step out, the air biting my hot skin. The mirror's all fogged up, my own image a blur. I swipe it clean, seeing my eyes—dark, wild, just like the emotion she's stirring up inside me.

My body's a roadmap of scars, each one a tale of survival, a badge I wear with a kind of twisted pride. It's weird, this reflection staring back at me. I let my fingers trail over the jagged lines, the skin rough beneath my touch, a reminder of life's ruthless lessons.

The pain doesn't bother me; it hasn't in a long time. It's the emotions that mess me up, the ones I can't figure out for the life of me. Like now, I've got this feeling clawing at my insides, and I can't even put a name to it. All my life, I've been shutting down any shit that could make me weak, that could be used against me. Kill or be killed—that's the world I know, where pleasure is found in the finality of a bullet's path.

But here I am, taking a hard look at this guy before me, and I can't shake the fact that something's changed. Emotions—those fucking things I thought I had on lockdown—they're there, lurking, making me question shit I never used to. I've lived by the thrill of the hunt. When I kill, it's the rush that gets me, that high of having the power of life and death in my hands. Yet now, in the silence of my own bathroom, I'm feeling something else. Something that doesn't fit into the boxes I've built to keep myself safe and sane. And I don't like it. Not one bit.

It's like a foreign invader, and I'm standing here trying to identify the emotion that's got no place in my life. Is it fear? Hell no, I don't do fear. Is it doubt? I've never doubted myself before.

But right now, with the mark of my life's battles on display, I'm confronted with the undeniable truth that I might just be human after all. And I'm not sure I'm ready to deal with what that means.

I turn away from the mirror, from the reflection that seems like a stranger, and brace myself against the sink. The cold marble beneath my palms brings me back to the present, to the reality of who I am.

I don't do emotions. They're a liability, a weakness I can't afford. But as much as I try to shake this feeling, I know that somewhere along the way, the game has changed. And I don't know the damn rules anymore.

After some hours of sleep, I get dressed, each move excited by the thought of round two. Wondering how much she'll push back, how far she'll go before she realizes she can't fight the fucking pull between us—it's a thrill.

The house is dead quiet as I roam the halls while every soul here is still asleep. I step out into the break of day, suck in a deep breath of that cold morning air. Lighting a cigarette, I walk back to my car. A Datsun 240z that I took great care to modify to my images during the years.

Aggressive, dark, and mysterious. The day's laying out in front of me, full of shit to do, and I can't shake this feeling that Fallon's going to fuck up the balance I've got here. A smirk twists on my face. Bring it, bunny. Let's see what you're made of, let's see if you can actually handle Camden fucking Betto.

Barreling through the scorching wasteland of Death Valley, the desert blurs into a relentless haze as I floor it, the speedometer's needle in a relentless climb.

I veer off onto a hidden track, a secret only a handful of us know. The Datsun's tires rip into the earth, sending clouds of rock and dust ballooning out behind like the aftermath of an explosion. This godforsaken place is harsh and ruthless, but it's precisely where I have to be.

This relic of a building stands up ahead, all battered by time and the ceaseless beatdown from the desert. I kill the engine, and suddenly, it's just the silence of the wasteland, punctuated by my thudding pulse and some distant, pained howls sneaking out from a nearby container.

I step out, the ground scorching beneath my boots. I stalk over to the container, the metal burning to the touch. Hinges scream as I wrench the door wide. Inside's a guy, tied down and looking about ready to lose his mind. Panics got him by the throat, sweat carving through the filth on his face.

The knife in my grip is like an old friend. My skin's feeling the sear inside this tin coffin, and the air's heavy with dread and waiting. Each step closer cranks the voltage up a notch. The game's different here; this is my damn turf. "Why isn't Bob nowhere to be found?" I ask, my irritation evident in my tone.

"I' don't know! I swear," he stammers, tears spilling from his eyes. I hurl the knife with all the force I can muster. It makes a sickening sound as it embeds itself deep into his knee, eliciting a primal howl of agony from him. Leaning in, I press my face close to his, brushing away a loose strand of hair that had tumbled onto my brow.

"Speak up, or I swear I'll lose my patience, and you don't want that," I growl, the threat hanging heavy in the silence.

The quiver in his eyes tells me he's on the brink, scrambling for words that might save his skin. "Out with it," I snarl, allowing him to spill the truth off his tongue one last time. "He... he might've gone to Thailand... for collecting," he stammers, each word steeped in dread. Pathetic.

He's served his purpose, and now he's just a useless piece of meat. I seize him by the hair, wrenching his head back with a forceful yank. My other hand finds his throat, and in the next heartbeat, I drag the blade across the skin, the crimson cascade splattering against me, a grotesque baptism that I live on a regular basis. My favorite fucking color.

The steel confines reverberate with the aftermath of the turmoil, a stark reminder of the carnage just enacted. I emerge, remnants of savagery stubbornly adhering to my flesh like grotesque armor, the tang of blood and terror saturating the air.

The gruesome scene I leave behind is my mark, a communiqué penned in the dialect of my father's dark dealings. Extract the outstanding dues, seize the asshole trying to play in our back, and claim their very essence if need be.

I seal the container with a resolute slam, ensnaring the echoes of a man's last gasps, a fool who dared defraud the enterprise by protecting a fucking man no more important in this world than a cockroach. My work in this place is concluded, yet the mission extends beyond here. The target of my pursuit, Bob, has racked up a debt as vast as the stars to my dad, believing he can elude fate in the far reaches of Thailand.

My duty to Franco is unambiguous. I am the reaper, an unyielding omen that obligations to the Betto family don't simply vanish into the ether. I collect what is ours, be it currency, merchandise, or vengeance, executing my father's decrees with icy precision. And when the moment demands, I extinguish existence. I settle into the driver's seat, the leather greeting me like a partner in countless past indiscretions. I need to go to the airport and fly in the jet to Bangkok. There's solace in the thought that Fallon may run for her life somewhere far from here. I feel something like possession for her. I don't like the idea of letting my bunny in the snake den without me to protect her in the shadows. It's peculiar, the bond I've formed with that creature.

CHAPTER 6

FEELING

FALLON

The days stretch on, long and monotonous—boring life, boring place. A quiet unease settles over me more each day that passes, a sense that the mansion masks something more sinister than I first thought.

The comings and goings of strangers in Franco's office, whispers of clandestine meetings late at night, and Franco's fleeting presence add to the house's mysterious rhythm. My days are a carousel of idleness—turning in circles, going nowhere. I almost finished the book-lined shelves of the library. Yet, the words are mere distractions. It's so boring having nothing to do.

The mansion's silence is heavy during the day, a tapestry that mutes the underlying tension. In the stillness, I sense the dissonance—a veneer of normalcy that fails to convince me. One evening, over dinner, I told Franco and Valentina that I needed to find something to do, some purpose, because just floating around without a plan drives me nuts.

Franco, with his ever-calculating gaze, offered me a role to manage the social media for his association. I grabbed this chance, a job that might help me understand the mystery of this weird family and fill my days.

I started looking all over the mansion for any papers or tiny bits of information that could help me find something meaningful. But I didn't find anything.

A week has passed since the last night I saw my stepbrother, and Camden remains a specter. The solitude breeds a strange mixture of relief and disappointment.

My quest for something important leads me down halls today, each room another piece of the puzzle, another fragment of the Betto mystery. The mansion breathes with a life of its own, its secrets tucked away in shadowed corners and behind locked doors. I will carve out a space for myself within these walls, I swear, if it means finding the reason my guts have twisted since I'm here.

In the quiet solitude of a dark room that looks like storage, I think of Camden—his absence sharpens the image of him in my head. What keeps him away? What occupies his time at night? The questions multiply, and my hunger for answers only seems to grow with them.

My resolve to uncover the truth is set. After all, what is a mansion but a house of cards waiting for the slightest breeze to reveal its hand? And I will be that wind. The storm outside is loud and wild. It's very late, the time when everything is so quiet, waiting for the night to end and the morning to begin. I sit by the window in my room, trying to get lost in a book. The cold glass pressed against my face as I read. But even though I'm looking at the words, the noise of the thunderstorm gets my attention. They sound far away, like a lost warning, and every time lightning flashes, it's as if the night jumps, showing us what it's hiding for just a second.

I feel a chill, and the hair on my neck stands up. That creepy feeling like someone is watching me, following every move I make without making a sound. The book slips from my hands as I look into the dark outside.

Suddenly, whether by luck or some trick, a bolt of lightning lights up the sky, and for a moment, its brightness shows a shadow, a man standing outside in the rain. He's not hiding from the storm or looking for a place to stay dry. He's literally just standing, looking at me through the rain. Camden.

He stands, looking scary down there, the rain hitting his broad shoulders, his clothes wet, his hair sticking to his forehead. He doesn't move or seem scared when the thunder booms. He is watching me quietly from below; his look is as heavy as the thick clouds above.

I can't move. I stop breathing, and my head is trying to figure out why he's there, stalking me in the damn rain.

The lightning disappears, hiding Camden's shape and returning him to the dark. But I can still see him when I close my eyes. I can feel the storm inside my own traitorous body, stirred up by him, by the silent way he seems to claim me as he watches from the wet grass.

I know we're in a silent face-off, and with the thunder as my only company, I can't stop looking at the spot where he stood, where he's still waiting.

I'm sure he'll be there again when the sky lights up. But he is no longer there when the light finally strikes the ground again.

I decide to get up and take a shower. Ice cold. To take my mind off this weird night. Thunder grumbles in the distance, an ominous symphony to the night's unrest.

I stand beneath the torrent, surrendering as rivulets forge haphazard trails across the landscape of my skin, converging at my waist before submitting to oblivion. My palms glide across the contours of my body. Desperate for distraction, I summon thoughts distant from Camden. I try.

Lathering soap on my skin, fragrance blossoms in the steam's embrace, camellia's sweet nectar mingling. I allow my eyes to fall shut, enshrouded in this sensorial veil, only to sense an intrusion, a weight, imperceptible yet smothering. With a whip-like snap, I pivot, heart galloping in my chest. Through the misted glass, an apparition forms.

He stands, drenched, his gaze piercing through the vapors, a ghost conjured from steam. Shock swiftly surrenders to silent confrontation. I will not succumb or display vulnerability.

With a posture that shows both resistance and a quiet recognition of the upcoming conflict, I present myself to him, unshielded, fearless. My body does not falter, nor do I seek hiding. I am a statue of poise. Eyes interlocked with his, a brave display of determination and openness combined.

Our scene is filled with silent promises and risks, a delicate dance on the edge of danger. His breath breaks the silence, shallow and hard. I swear I saw a smirk just now on his lips. In my stillness, conflicting sensations battle within me, the hot against the cold. The crave to let him look at me longer and the need to turn around and hide my body. I contemplate the risk of both options, wondering how deep I will go and what price I'll pay. "Cover yourself, sister." His words are rough, and I laugh at the nerve of his demand.

"You're the one in MY bathroom, stalker."

He doesn't move, but I can see his jaw clench and the anger rising in his eyes. I am completely lost. What the fuck was he thinking was going to happen?

"Still here, I see." He says, relaxing his shoulder just a notch.

"Wow, he has eyes, the bastard." Mocking sneer colors, my voice edged with a sharp venom bite.

With deliberate caution, I extend my hand towards the showerhead, maneuvering it with a subtle grace to nestle between my thighs. Does he believe his intimidation and scare tactics can shake me?

He's about to learn a swift and stern lesson. I softly moan with pleasure at the sensation of the water stream hitting directly on my clitoris while maintaining steady eye contact with him. He looks like he's about to implode from the inside. "One day, bunny, you're going to regret this." And with that, he leaves.

Despite the extravagance oozing off the walls of this fortress of a home, the gnawing tension in my gut remains unshaken. Striding across the gleaming floors, my mother approaches me, her touch barely skimming my arm.

"Fallon, darling," her voice lilts, equal parts dismissive and warning, "This isn't just some party. It's the annual charity gala of the Betto Association. " As she readies the place with the employees for the imminent gathering, the ambient sounds fill the room. The distinct clink of porcelain plates being handled, and the gentle swish of silk fabric serve as rhythmic punctuation to her meticulous preparations.

Each movement and sound contribute to the atmosphere, creating a sense of anticipation for the approaching event. The delicate interplay of these sensory details hints at the care and attention she dedicates to ensuring everything is just right for the forthcoming affair.

Excitement and grandeur saturate the air, mingling with the sting of her pricey scent. My eyes sweep the expansive dining hall that will host the spectacle, picturing the power players who'll fill it, those shadowy figures pulling strings from afar. The notion sends an involuntary shudder through me, even as the call of the uncertain tugs at me.

Franco's voice shears through my thoughts, its sharpness a stark reminder of what's at risk. "Bear in mind, Fallon," he intones, power oozing from every syllable, "All the high and mighty will be there to feast, swill, and... partake in a spot of genteel betting for a good cause."

A smile plays on my lips, all rehearsed charm, but it does nothing to ease the leaden sensation his words stir up. The gala's just a charade of goodwill, where relics with stories as gilded as their price tags will exchange hands in the spirit of giving. Yeah, way to buy a conscience.

Franco and Mom lock eyes in the briefest moments, a wordless exchange that sidelines me. Franco drives his point home, a thread of finality through his speech, "This night is massive for us, for you. Grasping the importance of this occasion and your place in it is crucial." His words hang there, a cloaked admonition that spells out just how precarious my footing is in this world of theirs.

I give a nod, my promise of obedience, but inside, my head's abuzz with questions and a mounting sense of rebellion. What ugly truths are behind the facade of generosity? Can I manage to slip away unnoticed? And the real kicker is, will Camden be there?

Mom's laughter rings out, hollow, and joyless, as I turn away, the shadow of the approaching night pressing in on me. Franco's eyes cling to me, silent and watchful, his gaze a dare and an order rolled into one.

The well-kept lawn spreads before me, bathed in the gentle touch of the fading sun, providing a brief escape. I stroll along the stone path, the vibrant flowers trying to capture my attention. Surrounded by greenery, even if just for a moment, I can imagine being untouchable here, away from the mansion's chilly glamour.

At the heart of it all, the pool shimmers, mirroring the ever-shifting gaze of the heavens. The surface dances with the breeze, art alive and fleeting.

Her heels hit the ground like a metronome to my

thoughts, and without a glance, I know she's near. The embodiment of cutting grace, Valentina moves in with her calculated strides. Her scent, a concoction of floral notes and relentless drive, wraps around me with the soft wind.

"Something's off, Mom," the words slip out, half-lost to the whispering leaves, "it's Franco. Can't shake the feeling."

She halts, her perfect features creasing with vexation. She brushes off my words with an air of impatience as though swiping at a pesky fly. "Dear, you're being overly anxious. Why not indulge in some retail therapy? There's a gala tomorrow, and you need to look the part." Her hand appears, a card as dark as night between her fingers. "Franco's orders," she says, her lips pulling up into a gigantic grin. "Use it as you wish. There's no limit. Just go have fun." Even as the card shifts from her grip to mine, a silent message lingers between us, the air tinged with her irritation. It's light in my hand, yet it bears down on me with expectation, a bribe laced with silent consent to the man I can't trust.

The cold bite of its surface against my skin starkly defies the warmth around us. There's an itch under my skin for something real, a craving for something authentically mine. Escaping this cage for just a heartbeat is my first move.

Daniel's my ticket to town. My mission? A dress. But not just any dress. I yearn for something that reflects the rebellion simmering inside me: a sleek, black gown, a shadow to wrap around my defiance.

I find him elbows deep in the hood of a car, and I cut straight to the chase. "Daniel, I need to get into town. I have to pick up a dress." He pauses, wiping his hands with a rag, an intrigued arch to his brow. "Certainly, Miss Fallon. Which ride would you prefer?"

I turn my gaze to the left, and a row of luxurious opulence stands before me. However, amidst the dazzle, one car beckons to me, the dark grey vehicle that caught my eye upon our arrival. Its somber aura resonates with the mood that envelops me, drawing me closer.

I point, my decision instant. A laugh, rough as sandpaper, breaks from Daniel. "That's impossible," he says, almost under his breath. I snap at him, the annoyance etching into my features. "And why's that?"

He carefully measures his following words before leaning, "That's Camden's car." The name sends a spark to my core, igniting a dangerous thrill—Camden's ride. The knowledge feels like a new challenge. It's a new side quest for me. A little flirt with the inferno. I wonder how he would react.

Daniel holds my gaze, a silent observer of the whirlwind of defiance brewing in my head. What exactly am I after? I question the wisdom of reaching for something so intimately linked to Camden and fuck with it.

"Alright then," I respond, my tone betraying none of the inner chaos. "Not that one." Even as I yield, my eyes linger on that taboo machine. Daniel nods of understanding. As we selected an alternate car, I stole one last glance. "What is that car?" I ask. "It's a Datsun. A beautiful one. Camden loves this car. It's the only one he wants to drive. " He tells me, smiling to himself. Somewhere in my soul, a promise takes hold. I will pilot that car one day.

As we glide through the cityscape, I glance at Daniel, whose profile remains steadfast as a sentry, hands expertly guiding the wheel. Unable to resist, I playfully nudge him. "Hey, Dany-boy, think you can navigate these streets as smoothly as you handle the Betto family secrets?" He grins, the corners of his mouth softening the stoic facade. "Smooth navigation is my specialty, but family secrets require an extra layer of finesse." I chuckle, enjoying the camaraderie. "You're the Betto family's secret weapon, huh?" Daniel winks, "Well, I do my best. But no." We share a low laugh, the subtle exchange a testament to the trust and affection woven into our journey together. "You ever get tired of chauffeuring people around town?" My voice breaks the cabin's sanctity once more. His eyes flicker to mine. "One could say it has its... moments," he responds, the vaguest hint of a smile dying before it blooms.

I lean back, the corners of my eyes crinkling, an ember of curiosity firing up. "Must give you an interesting view of the Betto's dealings," Daniel's grip on the wheel tightens almost imperceptibly, a small testament to the weight of the words unspoken. "One sees many things," he concedes, the statement hanging between us like a dangling thread I'm itching to pull.

The car slows at a red light, the rhythmic tap of my fingers on the armrest filling the space. "And Camden, what's his... occupation? He certainly seems to have his finger in many pies." For a moment, silence reigns, save for the metronomic tick of the turn signal.

Daniel exhales, a quiet release fraught with caution. "Mr. Betto's interests are... varied. His pursuits require a certain... discretion." A chuckle escapes me, laced with the thrill of dancing around the fire's edge. "Discretion. So he's the guardian angel of the family secrets?" The light shifts to green, and Daniel sends the car surging forward. "Miss Di Genova, our paths can often lead to... unexpected destinations. It's wise to be mindful of the direction we choose." His words sounded like a warning, forming a knot in my stomach. A veiled message that the waters I test may run more profound, more treacherous than I know. I press my lips into a thin line, gaze flickering to the passing scenery. "I'll keep that in mind, Daniel." The car veers onto a quieter street, leaving behind the vibrant hustle and bustle of downtown. Here, the city's rhythm softens into a subtle hush, replaced by an air of exclusivity that permeates the surroundings.

CHAPTER 7

BUNNY'S DRESS

CAMDEN

The engine's growl is my sole companion as I tail the car transporting Fallon, the sound rumbling beneath my feet like hell's lullaby. The sight of Valentina slipping Franco's card pissed me off.

It's almost as if he's trying to mark territory with her, but my instincts rebel against the notion. She's not his; she's mine. A primal, possessive surge courses through me, compelling me to assert my claim. It's a raw and domineering urge that controls me.

My fingers unconsciously clenching the steering wheel. She's not his to purchase, keep tabs on, or twist around his finger. That privilege is mine, solely mine.

When Daniel finally halts the car, my eyes are glued to her as she emerges. A fucking dress boutique, of course. I'm out and inside before my heart beats again.

I can't afford any uncertainty, not when she's part of the equation. And right there, in the midst of it all, stands my enchanting little bunny, bathed in the sunlight, draped in the elegance of silks and satins of the clothes around us. Her delicate fingers dance over the fabric of a gown, and against my better judgment, my imagination takes a detour.

I can clearly picture this damn gown sliding from her supple form, revealing her body to me. It's a tempting image that sends a jolt directly to my cock, stirring desires that had been carefully restrained.

I'm in my element, stalking my prey, the murmur of conversation, the seductive scent of fresh fabric. But my eyes are fixated on her. Surrounded by tulle and lace, she's a mesmerizing revelation that leaves me fucking breathless.

Franco believes his riches will bind her and hold her nearby. But he's got it twisted. I've put my eyes on her, and now I'll never look at someone else again.

Rooted to the spot, I'm fucking obsessed as she sifts through the array of gowns, each selection a testament to the defiance sparkling in her gaze. Watching Fallon trying on outfits, clueless of the predator lingering in the woods' shadow, reels me in.

I can nearly savor her, an exquisite blend of naivety and temptation that latches onto me, refusing release. She's oblivious, but she belongs to me, and I'll play dirty to keep it that way. I don't mind being the villain in her story if it means caging her in my arms.

I'm about to make my presence known when the atmosphere twists, hitting pause. A dress snags her eye, a black dress with little chains as straps. Her pick hits me like a stealthy blow to the gut. I'm thrown off balance, yet a grudging smirk creeps over my face.

Alluring, yet guarded. That's Fallon, a tantalizing siren unaware of the peril in her waltz. But I see it clearly. I'm wrapped up in it. She's mine. And no fancy card from Daddy dearest is about to alter that reality. "Hey, sis," my voice makes her jump as I sidle up to her. She rolls her eyes before shooting me a lethal glare.

"Why the hell are you here? Did you crawl out the floor like the insect you are?"

"I followed you." My blunt honesty throws her off balance.

Someday, I'll paint that pretty confused face with my cum. But for now, she needs to get the hell out of my sight. "When are you gonna fuck off?" I ask.

"Never, asshole. Now, back off, I'm shopping for a dress

for tomorrow."

Ducking behind a wall of fabrics, shielding myself from any prying eyes, I stealthily approach her. A deep, ominous growl rumbles from deep within me as I lock eyes with her, the intensity of my gaze loaded with a potent mix of desire and danger.

I close the distance, the air thick with a charged energy that transcends the realm of the ordinary. A guttural expression of primal instincts escapes my lips, a visceral proclamation of possession reverberating through the clandestine space between us.

With every inch, the atmosphere intensifies, a convergence of raw sensuality and the unmistakable undercurrent of a predator marking its territory.

I whip out my trusty knife, always hidden in my pocket. She's tough as nails and doesn't cringe a bit when I start to drag the blade across her skin, pressing just enough to leave a red mark down her arm.

Her eyes, those wild, amber jewels, don't budge, staying

fixed on mine. "You don't get the danger you're in." She swallows hard, but my little spitfire doesn't move. My blade, now teasing the valley of her breasts, I press the point, and she barely jumps. "You've wandered into a snake pit, little bunny. You're gonna get eaten alive. Run."

Her audacity steals the breath from my lungs as she inches closer, the sharp kiss of the blade biting into her skin, a crimson bead swelling at the puncture. My nerves ignite in alarm.

"Fuck you. I'm the snake. You and your fucked-up family are the bunnies." I'm smitten. I'm obsessed.

Pocketing my knife, I shamelessly admire her beautiful, now blood-streaked breasts. I whip out a credit card from the back pocket of my jeans and slip it into her cleavage. "Use this one." Before she can react, I snatch her handbag and hoist it out of her reach. She's so much shorter than me. It's hopeless for her. Fishing out her wallet, I yank out my father's goddamn card. She lands a punch right in my gut, knocking the wind out of me as I hand her bag back, grinning affectionately. "See you at tomorrow's Gala, bunny." I'm pacing like a wild thing stuffed in a box, the kind of seething rage bubbling up inside me that's just itching to blow. I charge into the old man's office like a goddamn hurricane, tearing through that space of hush-hush power plays. "Back the fuck off of Fallon!" I roar, my rage smacking against the walls decked out in dusty paintings of dead folks with their eyes glued to the shitshow.

I'm not clued in about his complete scheme yet, but I can feel it: dark things are scheming and plotting in hidden corners of his twisted mind.

Old Franco's just lounging there, smug as hell in his big-boy chair, and he has the nerve to chuckle. It's the kind of laugh that gives you the irresistible urge to punch him in the throat. "Know your damn place, son," he taunts. The crap weasel starts in on about the gala, that farce happening tomorrow where they all jerk each other off about how loaded and fake generous they are. "Watch your back," he barks at me. I'm supposed to be the watchdog, the monster. "Keep her out of your games," I say firmly. My hands curl into fists, tight as a vice. I'm just another chess piece to him, shoved around this glitzy meat market full of schmoozers too shit-faced to remember whose pockets they're in. I've always been an object to him, but I refuse to see Fallon suffer the same fate. The fury is like a blaze inside me, but I slap on my ice-cold game face because I know stepping out of line with him costs a hell of a lot. In this sprawling Betto kingdom, even the prince has gotta toe the line, or he's going down with the rest of the pawns. And I really never give two shit, but right now, something has changed. Someone, I can't fucking make a run for her damn life. Stubborn little thing.

CHAPTER 8

THE GALA

FALLON

The previous night passed without incident. I returned home with my new dress, satisfied. However, I had to shower upon arrival to erase all the bloodstains. I even had to hide my chest from Daniel to prevent him from seeing and asking questions. Tracing the faint line of my scar nestled discretely between my breasts, I reflect on the eerily cold sensation of Camden's blade. It's a mark most would never notice, but its presence is a stark reminder of a past fraught with pain. As I silently ponder over it, I realize Camden's eyes never caught the subtle indentation on my skin. Even when his eyes were burning my skin. The intimate proximity of his knife to my old scar had unexpectedly churned up a tide of long buried, harrowing recollections I thought I had forgotten. Flashback of myself as a toddler, a flashback that make me feel sad and terrified. But why? I don't know.

The reflection that gazes back at me is framed in the soft illumination of the makeup vanity mirror's bulbs, a gentle embrace casting warmth upon my features. My fingers, skilled and sure, add a swipe of rouge to my cheeks, sharpening the pallor of my complexion into vivid relief.

A subtle smirk curls my lips, echoing the daring in my veins. I'll use Camden's hovering vigilance as a weapon, wielding it with a sly grace. The buzz of this decision sends a thrilling shiver down my spine.

Carrying this secret adds gravity to the act. I'm attracted by the thrill of danger like a moth to the flames. My reflection stares back at me, one last scrutinizing look, and I rise from the chair, the sound of the chair's legs scraping the floor merging with the quiet around me. In this secluded space, I have transformed, and tonight, I emerge anew. I want to play with him.

As I walk down the giant staircase, each step is filled with a mix of nervousness and excitement for the night ahead. Dressed in a gown that unveils my curves, I'm met by a young woman in a dress that shows she's working at tonight's event, her young face barely hiding her unease. Her smile, made to look nice for guests, can't fully cover up a fear that mirrors my own secret worries.

She leads me to the start of the main room. Before me, the space opens up, filled with elegant people and quiet talk, smelling of gourmet food. I look around at the important people there; even though I'm not an expert in powerful connections, I can tell that the some are important. The arrangement of the tables reveals hierarchies and associations, as prominent flower decorations oversee discreet yet significant conversations and clandestine scheming.

My mother and Franco come up next to me, showing off their wealth and control. For a bit, I'm just another pretty thing on Franco's arm, saying hello to those who smile with their lips but not their hearts. I act the part, speaking sweetly, looking around playfully, my face showing calm politeness. A lingering sensation creeps over me as if unseen eyes are fixated on my every move. It's an unsettling awareness that there are observers hidden in the shadows, their gaze leaving me with a palpable sense of scrutiny. Or maybe just one.

Something inside me tells me to look around the room, and there, in the corner of the room, is Camden. Grand in his silence, he's the mystery in all the fake happiness, watching me. The inked serpent on his skin, stretching expansively over his chest, commands attention, especially as it peeks out beneath the casually unbuttoned shirt, left intentionally open for an effortlessly laid-back effect.

As the grand hall swells with the murmurings of the elite, I try to fade into my chair. Franco's booming voice cascades over the attendees, each word measured, each pause calculated to hang anticipation in the air. I watch him, the epitome of control, orchestrating the evening like a conductor with his symphony.

He directs the attention toward me in a hand gesture, and my name spills from his lips. In an instant, every eyes are on me. I become the selected new offering to the highest bidder in exchange for a dance. Nice to be auctioned off right after a mere clay vase. And without my consent.

The weight of the entire room on me; the rising bids seem to construct invisible shackles in the air around me. I search the crowd in a silent plea for mercy, for salvation from the auction block. My gaze flits to my mother, Valentina, whose concern flickers only briefly before she masks it. She knows this game all too well, the sacrifice of dignity for wealth's embrace.

Bidding wars are nothing new to this filthy rich, but when the offer hits one hundred thousand dollars. I can't help but feel like I've been priced at the value of my entire existence. The last bidder, a repulsive figure with his lecherous grin and corpulent frame, seems more beast than man. In the gleam of his eye, I see myself reflected, an object, nothing more, nothing new. A heavy sense of dread envelops me as if a stone has plummeted into the depths of my heart.

And then emerging like an avenging angel clad in darkness. With his stature commanding silence, Camden raises his hand in a decisive gesture that freezes the whole room. His bid, a staggering fucking half a million, throws everyone into disarray. Even the oxygen seems to halt in the room, the sum echoing like a thunderclap against marble walls.

His gaze flickers to mine, a silent exchange in the chaos. I don't want to show him my relief. Instead, I roll my eyes. Why would I give him the fun to know he saved my ass. But the truth is, his intervention is a twisted lifeline, an embrace that is both shield and shackle. The room erupts in a cacophony of reactions. I find myself standing at the crossroads of frustration and fascination, my fate now inextricably tied to Camden.

As the auction ends, I stand up with the rest, eager to leave behind my fake interest in the fancy items they were selling. I walk rapidly but quietly, moving past groups of people, laughing, and talking. Dodging a server with a tray of shiny glasses of bubbly drink, I want to escape and be alone, ragging in a hot bubble bath about this night and Franco.

But as I'm almost out of the room, a large hand grabs my wrist. It's a firm hold that turns me around. I gaze directly into Camden's eyes. Their deep blue hue has a captivating effect as if they have the power to draw me in and lose myself within them. "You owe me a dance," he says in a low voice. It's like an order, but it sounds like he's asking simultaneously. My heart beats fast. I know I can't say no, not with everyone around now looking.

I try to pull away, starting to say no, but he cuts me off with a quiet but scary warning. "Be careful, bunny. Daddy's watching. You wouldn't want to upset him, right?" I let out a sigh. It's so quiet it's almost lost in the music that starts filling our ears.

I grit my teeth and trail behind him to the area where bodies sway, entwined in a slow dance. Camden's hand rests on my back, initially offering a pleasant sensation, but then his grip tightens, causing discomfort. Facade of friendliness and politeness outwardly, all while inflicting hidden pain that goes unnoticed by onlookers.

We dance smoothly across the floor, looking like another elegant couple. But it's all just for show. My foot hurts from the times I step on his on purpose. Every smile, every sweet look is just part of the act, and I'm stuck playing along against my will.

The gentle lighting accentuates his face's contours, rugged features, strong jawline, and incredibly smooth lips. I notice a few small white hairs on his beard. His gaze is so intense that it sends a thrilling sensation rippling beneath my skin. And once again, I find myself questioning my sanity for thinking my new stepbrother is so handsome. He pulls me close. The heat from his hand seeps through my dress, leaving me with a desire that feels almost too strong. Each move and twist makes me feel more connected to him as if our bodies are talking in a way words can't.

The music gets louder, and he holds me tighter, silently showing he's in charge of our dance, and I fight it with each breath I have. It's an intoxicating mix of strength and excitement that lights up my senses, making me wait for what will happen next. The firm way he leads me gives me a feeling of safety that doesn't match the danger he seems to bring. It's confusing but also thrilling.

His scent is a potent mix of spice and something that's just him, drawing me in like magic, making me want to be closer to him. I'm very aware of his breath on my cheek, a light touch that makes me want more. Our bodies move perfectly together, creating a deep, risky connection full of emotions I can't ignore. "Give me one good reason I should fight, bunny." I try to tilt my head back to look at him, attempting to comprehend the question he just asked.

But he presses his body completely against mine, placing his head on mine, and my eyes close gently, choosing to ignore his words. The tension around us feels about to break. The music ends, and we stay close a little bit too long, not ready to break the connection. With a soft promise that remains in the air, we finally separate, knowing that something important has changed between us, tying us together in that dance.

CHAPTER 9

DADDY'S OFFICE

FALLON

As the fancy party fascinates the guests with its charm and shallow chit-chat, I use the chance to slip away unnoticed. I creep away with care, making my way through the winding hallways of the big house.

I remember the places where the security cameras can't see, which I've learned from paying close attention during my time here, so with careful planning, I go into an office, a different from the big room where Franco works during the day, this is a room where quiet talks and secret agreements happen away from people watching when his nocturnal guests come to visit him.

The office exudes a sense of constraint, considerably smaller in size than the other. A tangible weight hangs from the grand mahogany desk that centers the room or the commanding crimson carpet stretching beneath. Towering bookshelves, filled with secrets bound in leather, stand sentinel along the walls. To my right, an army of precisely organized filing cabinets caught my attention. I extend my hand, trying to coax one open, only to encounter the unyielding resistance of a locked drawer. Damn.

"You lost, bunny?" Camden's voice slices through the quiet, a low rumble that sets my nerves jangling and my heart thumping wild against my ribs. It's unexpected, the way he pops up. I'm suddenly all hyper-aware of him, his hulking presence just a flicker of shadow away from me. How the fuck?

I spin around, my breath hitching. I've got to try to look cool and collected. But it's hard, with him standing there, all broad and intimidating, closing the distance between us with slow, deliberate steps. The atmosphere crackles with an eerie, charged sensation that reminds me of the peaceful moments before lightning cleaves the sky. I find myself retreating on reflex, craving distance in the dim illumination. Peering through the half-light, I attempt to discern Camden's expression, yet it remains veiled in obscurity, rendering him an enigma shrouded in allure, and... Fuck, there's an undeniable, perilous magnetism to him.

His proximity is invasive, a deliberate encroachment on my space that sends a shockwave of heat scorching through my veins. The chill of the floor seeps through my shoe's little protection, a stark contrast to the warmth emanating from his towering form. I draw a shaky breath, an attempt to quell the pounding in my chest that threatens to break free.

The scent of his cologne envelopes me, an intoxicating fusion of worn leather and an exotic spice that's undeniably his, stirring an unfamiliar yearning within me. His gaze locks onto mine with predatory precision, and I jut my chin upward in a brazen act of defiance. It's not courage that fuels my stance. It's a vehement refusal to reveal the trepidation that he's somehow stirred to life within me.

"Yes, I got lost," I managed to whisper.

"Bullshit." I can't quite read the expression on his face, but the corner of his mouth twitches, like this game, amuses him that we've found ourselves in.

My lips parted, a sharp retort poised on the tip of my tongue, but the words died there, unsaid. His eyes lock onto mine with an intensity that pierces through me. It's a look that knows too much, stripping away my defenses and stirring a tumult of desire and unease within me.

Camden's voice finally cuts through with a husky timbre that drips with menace, trailing over my senses and leaving a trail of involuntary tremors in its wake. "What are you doing here? Searching for the serpent's head?" He leans in so close I can feel his breath tickling the skin of my forehead. It's weirdly calming, totally the opposite of the chilly marble of the office I'm gripping onto for dear life. Being this up close and personal, it's messing with my head, blurring everything else out until it's just Camden and me and my heart thumping away like crazy. "It's just the beginning, my little bunny."

For the first time, I'm scared of him. As his body presses against mine, I feel my chest crush tighter against him with every breath I take. His tongue swipes across his lower plump lip as my gaze locks with his, burning with an intensity that threatens to set me on fire totally.

His palm applies steady pressure on the minor wound his dagger has left on my skin, just above my heart, and my eyes inadvertently follow the trail his fingers make. "I wasn't expecting that from you," He smirks slightly, "Seems my bunny has a bite that's sharper than anticipated." His tone shifts, annoyance lacing his words, "And that's fucking irritating." Camden's laughter rings hollow in the tense air, the sound grating against my already frayed nerves. I can hear the amusement in it, dark and twisted. "Run, bunny," he taunts, his voice slicing through the chaos unfurling around us. His mouth is hoovering on mine, barely touching.

My heart hammers in my chest, each beat an echo in my ears as I sprint around the desk, a desperate attempt to put distance between us. The room blurs as I move, objects losing their form to become streaks of color whirling around me. His footsteps echo mine, a relentless predator closing in on his prey. Seizing my arm with a sudden grip, I react instinctively, and my fist connects solidly with his face.

The blood from his lower lip is a stark red smudge on his skin. It's the evidence of my desperate struggle against him, yet he wears it like a badge of honor, a mocking tribute to the violence we've found ourselves entangled in. I'm gasping, my breaths coming in shallow bursts as I feel his presence looming ever closer.

My hands grasp the edge of a little table, papers and trinkets crashing to the floor in my wake. "Run, bunny," he repeats, the words a snarled whisper that prickles at the nape of my neck—a lullaby from hell.

Then his hands are on me, solid and unyielding. He pulls me back with savage force, causing my feet to slip from beneath me.

I hit the floor hard, the impact reverberating through my skull as I landed. A shock of pain lances through my head, lights sparking behind my closed eyelids. The weight of his body atop mine is suffocating, his power an inescapable force. I feel his arousal pressing against my stomach, a disturbing intrusion against the torn fabric of my dress. A raw sense of vulnerability courses through me, a primal fear that fuels my adrenaline. And I try to kick, punch.

"I bet you're all wet between those perfect legs." Damn it, he's probably correct. The rush, the sharp sting of pain, the sheer thrill, it's all converging on my throbbing core. Because even though he's trying to intimidate me, and it's working, I can also see in the depths of his piercing blue eyes that he won't truly harm me. I can't explain it. I just know.

With sheer willpower, I manage to deliver a knee to his groin, the connection sending a wave of relief through me. He grunts, the sound a mix of surprise and pain, and in that fleeting moment, I scramble up. But freedom is short-lived. As I attempt to flee, he grasps the carpet beneath me and yanks it with a violent tug.

My body is thrown off balance, my surroundings spinning as I fall again. The back of my head smacks against the hard floor. Stars explode across my vision, a constellation of pain that anchors me to the spot.

He crawls above me again, a shadow that envelops me whole. I'm trapped, his form an oppressive shroud that suffocates all escape attempts. All I can smell is the scent of his blood. All I can feel is the weight of his body and the hot rush of my own blood, pounding in my ears, a drumbeat of impending doom.

Panting, the space between us hushes to a fleeting truce. A reckless urge simmers within me, tempting me to graze his lip with my teeth to claim a kiss. I'm a whirl of contradictions. His breath comes in ragged draws, his features mere inches from mine.

Deliberately gentle, his hand cradles my face, banishing errant curls from my cheek and tucking them tenderly behind my ear, settling on the tender spot at the back of my head. "Are you ok?" The question disarms me, an absurdity in its innocence.

My brow furrows in bewilderment, wrestling with his abrupt shift in demeanour. "Are you for real? You're a psycho. It's your fault I'm in pain."

His grin unfurls a genuine expression that looks like mischief, sending a treacherous skip through my pulsing pussy. Fuck it, he's got this smile that just grabs me. A droplet of blood trickles from his lips, swirling into my mouth, and instead of revulsion, something primal urges me to close my mouth and taste it, craving the metallic tang. "You are one terrifying bunny." He breathed out. Camden's strong arms encircle me firmly, steadying me as my feet meet the ground. The sudden, compassionate touch rattles my senses. I look up at him, finding a flicker of concern cutting through the chiseled stoicism of his features. "Hospital?" he asks, the word hanging between us, dense and filled with unspoken tensions.

A cold shiver races down my spine, the word alone sending my mind hurtling back through time. Small and frightened, my hands gripping the sterile sheets of a hospital bed. The stark white walls close in around me, and the medicinal smells mingle with the scent of fear. I swallow hard, the present and past colliding violently. The adult Fallon stands in Camden's careful grasp while the child Fallon trembles in the shadowy recesses of memory.

"No," I manage to choke out, my voice barely above a whisper, the anxiety of my youth bleeding into the dark complexities of now. Camden's gaze searches mine, tracing the contours of my visible distress. Perhaps he sees the flicker of that five-year-old girl within my eyes, vulnerable yet veiled by the passage of years. His brows knit together, a silent question forming as he gauges all my physical reactions.

My past haunts me, grasping with icy fingers, but I don't want Camden's care to be the thing that pulls me under. Especially since I don't really remember it, he doesn't press further. Instead, his arms retreat but remain poised, a ghostly presence ready to catch me if I falter.

As the silence stretches like a tightrope beneath our feet, I take a tentative step back, reclaiming the distance and the semblance of control it brings. I'm left standing at the edge of a precipice, one wrong move away from plunging into the depths. I can't escape the inevitable pull of my past or the gripping tension Camden weaves around me. But for now, all I want to do is lie in bed and die. Just fucking die.

"I will send the housekeepers right away to clean up our mess. We don't want Daddy to know we've come here." Something in his tone, in his face, tells me he's worried. And with one hand running through his beard, he leaves the room.

Fucking bruise, but freshly out of the shower, I find myself standing alone in the solitude of my room. The noise from the gala below becomes a distant murmur, almost a memory. Outside my window, the night presses its dark face against the glass, a silent keeper of whispered secrets and untold stories.

Peering out into the night, my gaze sweeps over the shadowy expanse of the estate's grounds. I observe the dwindling number of guests as they depart, their silhouettes disappearing into the darkness. Yet amidst the ordinary, an anomaly catches my eye: a lone figure clothed in black beside the garage, an enigmatic presence in the stillness of the evening.

A silhouette emerges from the inky depths, its face obscured by the ghastly grin of a skeleton mask that casts an eerie chill in the night. Rooted to the spot, it melds with the midnight gloom, unseen by the unsuspecting souls who wander nearby. In its grasp, something reflects the moonlight. I looked closely at my windows, thinking it's a big plastic bag.

Panic surges within me, my pulse quickening as a torrent of alarm and foreboding floods my senses. Squinting hard, I try to make out what the heck this person's up to. Holding my breath, I catch them sneakily cracking open the back of some shady-looking big truck. Oh fuck. A corpse. A shuddering gasp escapes me as the creature, a macabre spectre with cream bones, twists its head, gazing upward toward the mansion's highest spires—my damn room's window.

I jump on the floor, scurry, crab-like, beneath my bed, camouflaging myself amongst the dark. Silly, considering he's outside.

Sobs wrack my body, the bitter realization settling in like frost; I'm in a nightmarish hellscape with no escape in sight. And once again, I delve into my darkest thoughts. Why do I persist? Why do I have to witness this? I can't do it anymore. Life is too fucked up for me. I have nothing and no one.

CHAPTER 10

WRONG DATE

CAMDEN

Looking out over the empty desert of Death Valley, my boots are totally caked in dirt from this godforsaken place. The wind's howling something fierce, whipping my hair into a wild mess while I mull over tonight's dirty work.

Gotta be precise and have patience; it's just how I roll. Made sure the guy didn't even peep before I took him apart, piece by piece, leaving him to bleed out.

I'm standing watch as this big, dark container looms like a tomb, holding the leftovers from the grim job I just pulled off. Hauling the guy's dead weight is a real workout, but it's nothing compared to the heavy load of hate and obsession I'm lugging around and dumping the body into its temporary resting place that thumps when it hits the bottom. The smell of blood sticks to me like a nasty reminder of the savagery that's pretty much a part of who I am now. The deserts like an old pal, keeping all my sick little secrets and never breathing a word.

Clanging shut the container, the noise cuts through the silence, putting a pin in another crazy chapter in my search for some peace. But peace? Yeah, it's playing hard to get. This little getaway of mine in Death Valley is just a short break before I'm dragged back into the grind. Franco's orders are buzzing in my head, loud as the desert wind. Especially since I just killed one of the last distributors of his. He'll for sure send me on a mission to find another one. I sink into my ride. The steering wheel's icy to the touch, but it fits in my hands like it's made for me.

The wheels chew up every mile, and my obsession gets stronger, like a bad taste I can't shake. Fallon. Her fucking face is stuck in my head, uninvited. I can't shake the need to see her, to push her buttons, to stir the pot. It's like a craving that's digging its claws in deeper every time we clash. She's getting under my skin in a way that's messing with my head, throwing a wrench in my usual game.

She saw me tonight. I know she did. And I could tell she was freaking out. But I also know that my girl's drawn to the darkness like a moth to a fucking flame. I've let her watch me. It's impossible for her to know it was me, and I'm going to keep it that way. Going to spring a surprise on her real soon. If she's not going to bail to safety, I will go ahead and claim her, pull her in to unleash her full potential, and protect her.

I can't get rid of this creepy chill that's taken up residence in my bones. My ride grinds to a stop at this eerie dock. All swallowed up by shadows sticking out against the pitch-black water like some grim painting. The place always feels like shit. Once you know what kind of stuff passes here, you can't live like a normal being.

I get out; the night hits me with a blast of sea air, the wind howling like it's crying out for help, mixing with the clanking chains and sad cries coming out of the containers. Can't do anything about that now. I keep my straight face on heading for the dude transporting the merchandise here. He's calling the shots, dealing with all the stuff that comes and goes at this never-sleeping dock.

"How much today?" I ask. "Twenty grand boss. It's not as much as usual, but it's real quality. " We do our business quick, no small talk. I hand him an envelope stuffed with hush money, the kind of dough that talks way louder than anything. His sharp gaze locks in on mine as we confirm the details for the next drop-off.

But it's not the shipment that's got me all twisted up—it's thinking about what—or who—might be locked up in those metal boxes. I've got this nasty taste in my mouth that won't go away. I keep thinking about the women and kids, their lives in the hands of my soulless dad. It eats at me, this feeling of total crap. Sometimes, I wonder who I was before this world broke my heart.

"Everything's done, Mr. Betto." His voice cuts through my thoughts. I barely hear him, my head filled with all the images of him, the possibilities, and how soon it will be his turn to pass between my knives. How hard will he cry for mercy?

"Yeah, just make sure it gets there," I mumbled, shoving the rest of the cash at him, my other hand balled up tight like it's fighting the urge to fucking scooping his eyeballs right now.

I head back to my car, dragging the heaviness of this place with me—the promise I made to myself a long time ago in my mind.

The worn wooden door creaks as I push it open, stepping into the dimly lit bar. Each step I take feels heavier than the last, a tangible weight pressing down on my shoulders, pulling me deeper into a place of introspection I've never really spent time in. I make my way to the worn leather stool at the bar, its surface cool beneath my fingertips. With a practiced ease, the bartender slides a glass my way, amber liquid shimmering in the low light. As I take a sip, the fiery burn trails down my throat, momentarily distracting me from the relentless thoughts that have consumed my mind.

Around me, people engage in animated conversations, their laughter echoing against the backdrop of music, zandros, obsessed playing in the background. But despite the sensual atmosphere and the shit tonnes of fuckable girls here, I feel disconnected, lost in a maze of my own making.

Suddenly, a subtle shift in the room catches my attention. A woman, striking in appearance with cascading waves of raven hair and piercing eyes, begins to make her way toward me. Her steps are deliberate, each movement exuding confidence and allure. Her breaths bouncing from left to right, menacing to fucking jump out her cleavage. As she draws nearer, her gaze locks onto mine.

She leans in her perfume, a heady mix of jasmine and musk, intoxicating in its intensity. "Hey babe, what a beautiful man like you do here alone? " I look at her, bringing the rim of my glass to my lips.

Normally, I wouldn't speak, take her ass in the toilette, roughly, without word or damn emotions. A way to empty my balls. She's beautiful, but as I watch her, a summoning of newfound clarity crashes through me; I turn away, my voice firm and resolute. "Not interested," I assert, my words cutting through the smoky haze. "Leave me be."

Her eyes widen in surprise, a fleeting expression of disbelief crossing her features. Without waiting for a response, I rise from the stool, the weight of my decision settling in. The night air greets me as I step outside, offering a brief respite from the stifling atmosphere inside.

Making my way inside the mansion, each step feels like a battle, the weight of the evening pressing down on me. I reach my bedroom and collapse onto the bed.

Darkness envelops me, slowly pulling me to sleep; a single thought lingers on golden hair strands.

I roll out of bed, every muscle rebelling. The fucking alarm of the security camera from the door that separates me and my dad's wings wakes me up, and now I'm in a fucking bad mood. I stalk over to the desk; the moment the screen lights up, I see Fallon trapped between some asshole kid who's got only one thing on his mind, fucking what's mine. My blood boils as he tries to pin her down with his lips on the door leading to my side of the manor, but she's a fierce one.

I'm coiled tight, ready to jump in and make him regret he was ever born. But then Fallon's hand smashes into his throat, and I can't help but feel a twisted surge of respect and arousal.

She's feral, untamed, grinning like she's just won a goddamn war. Watching her stand her ground, I feel a burst of pride I didn't expect. I'm pissed off yet oddly impressed. She sparks something in me, an urge to protect.

That dickhead, he's just stirred up a fucking trained killer on his own ass. He doesn't know the depth of the shitstorm he's stepped into. I keep my eyes on her as he walks away, and slowly, the fire in my gut simmers down to a sinister smirk. He thought he could step on my rabid bunny and interrupt our silent, twisted dance, and now he's in for a world of pain. But that's a problem for later. For now, I sink back into my bed. I am dreaming of all the ways I'll make him pay.

The bone-white mask in my grip is emotionless and stark, the perfect mirror of the reaper I've morphed into, a phantom lurking just out of sight. I slide it on, its cold touch a fucked-up comfort, the empty sockets lining up with mine, morphing me into the merciless agent of agony. I spend my day sleeping, trying to rest my body for the first time in months. But tonight, I'm on the hunt.

My boot slams into the door, busting it off its hinges, the sound a fucking symphony to my seething rage. I step through the carnage of wood and splinters, the silence of his supposed safe haven about to crack and crumble under the sheer force of my fury.

I scan the room, full of disdain, fucking beige. There he is, caught off-guard, his face a canvas of horror. A twisted smile curls on my lips as I let my shotgun roar, the blasts slamming into each of his feet, pinning him down like a bug under my boot. His drop to the floor is music to my ears, his desperate howls are foreplay.

I drag his sorry ass, dumping his wretched body on the kitchen counter like some fucked-up offering to the gods of confession. My words are cold, hard as steel, as I growl, "What did you do to Fallon?" It's a demand ripped from the depths of hell, a guttural order for the godforsaken truth.

Spilling his guts, the sorry fuck weeps out, blubbering about some shit fling on a dating app, a morning coffee date with her, and I feel a surge of vile contempt coil in my gut. My hands act with a mind of their own, tearing off his filthy pants, the sound of fabric ripping as thrilling as his pitiful screams.

Before, he's nothing but a spineless naked worm, stripped and squirming. I press on with my questioning, my shotgun now a silent judge to the sins spilling out on this makeshift altar. Through the dead smile of my mask, I feast on the sight of him, drinking in his dread and the rank scent of his pure, undiluted fear.

It's a perverse rush. But as the piece of shit whimpers, the emptiness reverberates, a stark reminder of the bitter path that fucking dragged me to this moment. "I swear she was the one who started jerking me off in my ride. Once we got to her place, she didn't wanna keep it going." I put a merciless finger right in his right eye, pushing it back into his skull. His screams mix with throat sounds, the kind you make when the torture is too much to handle. "But you still tried." I tilt my head, looking at the now exposed hole in his face. "Please….please." I pull down his boxers, his sad dick limp. "So. She touched your dick?" I let out a crazy laugh.

"She will be punished for that. But you. You are going down tonight." Oh, bunny. You're about to find out that those hands won't be touching anyone unless it's me, even if it's for taking my life.

CHAPTER 11

QUESTION GAME

FALLON

The sun, bright and high in the sky, its light touches the surface of the pool with a warmth that feels warm and relaxing, a change I welcome after this fucking evening with that guy Andre. He was such a dick to me when I said I didn't want to sleep with him.

I swim through the water, my lazy strokes taking me to the side of the pool. I lift myself and lean my arms on the edge of the pool to rest my head on my hands, watching the garden workers as the garden helper carefully trim the tall bushes. Their clippers go through the green leaves, steadily cutting off the messy bits. The sounds of splashing and laughter that used to fill the public pool I was swimming in in Vancouver seem like distant memories, making me feel even more alone.

With all its beauty and size, this big, fancy house feels like a coffin. The water moves without warning, pulling me out of my thoughts. My heart misses a beat and I quickly turn to see what caused it.

There's Camden, moving through the water smoothly, which seems strange because he usually seems so intense and rough. His strong arms move with strength and careful control. The sun shines on his wet, dark brown hair, making him look casual. Almost like an average person. Perhaps behind the monster is a man. He gets closer, and the water splits for him as if he's controlling it without saying anything. He doesn't speak, focuses on closing in the space between us, and I can't help but hold my breath, waiting for him to get out of the water. He passes right next to me, our hands brushing under the water, and little pebbles run down my arms. His blue eyes fixed on mine so strongly, making my saliva hard to swallow. His gaze feels like a touch. "Enough with the mind games, Cam. Just tell me why you haven't given me a chance since I arrived. Damn, I could have called the cops on you so many times since I've lived here."

"Again. " He stops moving, stops breathing. "What? " I ask, confuse. "Say my name like that again, bunny." His tone is demanding, almost pleading. "Tell me why, Cam." A low growl escapes him, and he faces me, smiling. "Maybe because I know you love playing with me." His voice is confident.

The water wraps around us, a warm blanket that moves with us. Small waves, soft as a gentle push, touch my skin, pulling me into this strange place. Floating in the pool, I can really feel Camden near me, how he swims with easy, smooth movements, turning around me.

"Let's get to know each other right here, right now," I say out loud. My words are bold. The idea lingers between us, as exciting and risky as the man before me. He sided eye me quickly. "I don't do that. But, if you call me Cam again, I'll answer three questions." With each swim and kick, we get closer. I feel his eyes on my face and my neck, and I suddenly notice the really too-small white bikini I chose. My breasts squeezing together hides my scar just the way I want it to. I hate to see it. My nipples, now hard despite the warm temperature of the pool, are visible through the wet fabric. He watches me closely, like a hunter, making me feel a strong, raw need under my skin. "Cam. How old are you?" He bursts out laughing, and the sound almost makes me want to laugh back at him. "That's seriously the first question you want to ask me, pretty bunny? " I nod my head in certainty, and he shrugs his shoulders. "I'm thirty-five years old."

The water isn't just around us now. It feels alive with the energy we create together, like a clear, buzzing line connecting us. I can nearly feel it, even taste it, the strong tension. "What do you do for the enterprise? " I whisper my question and roll my eyes. I have no hope of him answering me. "I kill, I collect. And recently, I've been protecting my property." Camden moves viciously closer like the snake on his skin, quiet and careful, making my heart pound.

I'm aware of how I breathe. How my chest moves might show how much I'm feeling inside. I didn't expect him to be so honest. "Wow. OK. Are you really telling me that? Aren't you afraid that I'll go to the cops, FBI, fuck, even Interpol on you? "

"Oh, baby. You still have no idea how deep this sea is. And no, I'm not afraid that you'll denounce me. I'm fucking scared you'll rip my heart out while I sleep tho." The space gets so small between us that we're almost touching, almost crashing into each other. My senses are so sharp I can practically hear his heart beating with mine in a wild rhythm.

He stops just a few inches away from my face. Our eyes meet. We don't need words. I can see every small thing: his nose flares, his jaw tightens, and his lips part slightly.

Camden's hand comes out of the water, moving straight toward me. He touches my arm, lighting a hot trail on his path, and I can't breathe. Everything shrinks to that one touch where our skin meets. "Last question, bunny. " I swallow hard. "What exactly does the Betto enterprise do?" I have so many other questions. I wish I had the opportunity to ask them all. But he gave me three.

Without taking his eyes off mine, he enters the bottom of his face into the water and comes out gently, spitting a jet of water in my face like a fountain. And a voice coming from behind prevents me from taking revenge. "Camden! Get out of the pool." Franco's tone is terrifying, so angry.

I turn around, and his face reflects precisely the same things as his voice. "Don't talk about that anymore. To no one, not even Daniel." Cam whispers in my ear, sending chills all over my body. He uses his muscular upper body to pull himself out of the water in a single pull and walk away. What the fuck? Did Daniel tell Camden that I asked questions?

"Oh, bunny, I left you a present at the foot of your bed." He yells while walking. I stop breathing, my mind returning to the bloody rabbit. And I watch him disappear away beside his father.

CHAPTER 12

SNIP SNIP

FALLON

I walk rapidly through the halls, eager to go to my room and see what he is talking about. I can hardly breathe, feeling nervous and excited. When I open the door, the smell of lavender and clean sheets helps me relax, but I can't shake off the feeling that something terrible is lurking somewhere. I look around, trying to see if anything's messed up. A piece of white cloth on the floor catches my eye, and I quickly go to it with a pounding heart. The tissue has a red mark on it that looks like someone's blood. I reach out with shaky hands to touch it and feel that it's cold, the opposite of the warmth that's slowly leaving me because I'm so shocked. There's a note on the cloth, and the words on it make me feel shiver inside.

Bunny, you're mine. He thought he could touch you, so here's your revenge.

I open up the cloth, and there's a fucking dick. A DICK! I'm totally shocked and disgusted. I throw it on the ground. I know who it belongs to. It's from my last date.

What disturbs me most is that the sight of this weird offering does not disgust me as it should. The silence in the room feels heavy after this. And in all the confusion in my head. I picture Cam taking off this asshole little dick for me. But I am a big girl, not just a thing to be owned.

With my heart thumping, I take the piece of cloth and wrap the fucking penis inside it. I'm going to show him how I can play, too.

As I storm inside, the garage is a chaotic symphony of metallic scents and greasy textures. The fluorescent lights cast a stark glow on Camden's car. I feel it calling to me for retribution. I find Daniel cleaning the inside of a truck. "Dany-boy, I need you to leave, please," I demand, my voice as sharp as the urgency that's clawing at me from the inside out. I'm a ball of desperate energy, my skin prickling with the moment's intensity. "No can do, Miss Fallon," he mumbles, not even sparing me a glance as he continues his work. His refusal is a wall, but my determination is a hammer.

My hands tremble as I hold up the little thing wrapped in a white tissue. I wiggle the small package in front of Daniel's face, and he looks at the blood stain for a few seconds before finally looking me in the eye. His retreat is immediate, the quiet scuff of his boots against the concrete ground an echo in the suddenly empty space.

I breathe in surprise. No questions. So, he knows I'm the victim of Camden's madness. I duck under the chassis of the car. The scent of oil and rubber fills my nose, both pungent and oddly comforting, as I settle into my task, the focus of my thoughts narrowing to this singular act of sabotage.

A smirk curves my lips. The set of wire cutters is heavy in my hand, their steel jaws strong as I close them around the brake lines. The sound, a sinister whisper in the quiet garage. My laughter is a soft, private thing, sinfully sweet in its reflection of the chaos soon to unravel. Ah, the fucker will finally stop haunting me.

I twist back out and wipe my greasy hands on my jeans and place the dick in the passenger seat. My eyes glimmer, the scene playing out in my mind in vivid detail. Camden's realization, the horror, the helplessness as he drives to his doom.

I lick my lips, savoring the fantasy, a bitter tang of arousal for the power I wield with such a simple snip. The air around me feels thicker as I stand, the weight of my deed a tangible pressure against my chest. Each beat of my heart is a drumroll.

I slip out of the garage. The taste of revenge upon my tongue is sweeter than any forbidden fruit. As much as I would have really liked to wait, lying in a lawn chair near the entrance to witness the departure of my stepbrother, I have other cats to whip.

I decided to kick my ass and invest myself fully in my investigation of Franco. And what I want is paper, documents, anything tangible I can read or visualize. So I make my way confidently to his office, waving Daniel bye on my merry way.

"Hey, Franco, got a sec?" I pitch my tone just right, all casual and girly-like, trying to make it seems I'm here to chat about social media strategies or some such bullshit. That's my cover story, at least. He glances up, and I feel the weight of his suspicion. It's there, behind the polite mask, as he says, "Of course, Fallon, what's on your mind?" His eyes are sharp like he can see I'm playing a role just as much as he is.

I ease into my questioning, keeping it light. But all the while, I'm prodding, searching for a crack in his armor. I need a secret, something big, something that can give me leverage. The door behind opens and she walks in. Valentina, an interruption scripted by fate.

She plops down in his lap, all giggles and smoochy sounds with her soon-to-be husband, a display that's about as subtle as a gun to the face. While they're distracted, my eyes dash across the desk, scanning and searching. And fuck me, a paper that looks like a contract on Franco's desk catches my attention. *StarlightClub*. I file it away in my mind, a possible lead to somewhere. Valentina's kissing him, loud and sloppy, and I look at them with a disgusted face, walking back to the door.

The name *StarlightClub* is itching in my brain. I'm going to dig into this after dinner. There's a story there; I can feel it, and whatever it is, it's gonna be my ace in the hole.

As night falls, I sit at my vanity, slapping on some heavy makeup and getting all dolled up for the wild night ahead. When that endless dinner finally wrapped up, I bolted to my room, diving into my phone to scout out all the info about the club. Bam! In less than a minute, I've had the address.

Now, snagging the location is just step one. I need wheels, something slick and quick, without Daniel catching on. So, I sneak my way out of the house, tiptoeing like a ninja, making sure no one hears a peep.

The dim overhead lights flickered as I cautiously entered the vast garage. Rows of vehicles stood like silent witnesses. My eyes darted around, scanning the walls and corners for any sign of the keys I desperately needed. I approached a tall metal cabinet, its surface cool to the touch. Taking a deep breath to steady myself, I pulled open the cabinet's door, revealing a multitude of keys hanging from hooks. YES!

A particular set caught my eye. I reached out with a sense of intuition, grasping them firmly in my hand. Determined, I approached the car that lights up when I push the button on the remote. The soft gleam of its polished black exterior beckoned me closer—a compact BMW.

A surge of excitement coursed through me as I settled into the driver's seat, the car's contours embracing me like an old friend. With a turn of the ignition, the engine roared to life. With that address burning in my mind, this car, I hit the road, ready to dive headfirst into whatever the night throws my way.

I park the car a block away, the distant thump of bass already vibrating in the air, mingling with the city's pulse. Swiping on peachy gloss, I fluff up my wig, an intense contrast to my usual blonde color. I had to ask one of the maids for the Halloween costumes box, and she looked at me like I was the weirdest person ever.

Thank God I managed to outrun Daniel and take a car myself. The fucker never wants to let me go out without him, let alone bring me here. He would never have. StarlightClub's neon sign flickers, a beacon in the dark. My heels click against the pavement, every step an echo of the gnawing uncertainty that clings to me like a second skin.

I'm tugging on the hem of my skirt; it's way too short. Cursing my decision to dress so provocatively, yet knowing I need to blend in, not to stick out more than I already do.

The bouncer barely gives me a second look, his bored gaze sliding off me and opening the door. There's a sort of relief in that invisibility can be a blessing when you're stepping into such a scary place. As I step inside, I'm assaulted by a cacophony of sights and sounds, an overload to the senses. The thick air, with the musky scent of sweat and sweet perfumes, makes me nauseous.

The pulsing lights cast a kaleidoscope over naked women, moving with an almost hypnotic grace. I weave through the crowd and slip onto a bar stool, the leather cool and smooth under my thighs.

The bartender sidled over, and I ordered something strong, trying to emulate the nonchalance of the regulars. The glass chills my fingertips, condensation beading like tiny jewels. "Can I help you, sweetie? " My gaze turned to my left to find a young woman with black tape on her nipples smiling at me. "I'm the manager." She adds. "Oh, in that case, yes, you'll be a great help."

CHAPTER 13

IN TOO DEEP

CAMDEN

This bitch, my bitch. The growl of the engine thrums in my ears, a fierce cacophony that echoes the wild beat hammering in my chest. But there's a fucking hitch, no brakes. The pedal sinks beneath my foot, impotent, and a twisted grin splits my face. Isn't this a fucking bummer?

Earlier, in the dull glow of the garage, the sight of Fallon's gift tossed carelessly on the passenger seat should've set off alarms. A cute gesture, a deadly intent.

She had fucking sabotaged me, snipped the lines linking life to death. The recognition of her dark play sends a savage thrill through me, and my dick is so hard it could break granite. I have an insane appreciation for the lengths she's willing to go to. Fallon, my treacherous little bunny, aiming to end our game with a final, fatal strike.

Laughter bursts from my lips, raw and unhinged. Love. This is fucking love. The knowledge that she wants me dead sparks an inferno, a burning adoration fueled by her audacity. She's gutsy, my bunny, and that's a high I can't resist. Because I also know that she's not foolish enough to think this will work. She just wanted to play.

The car is a weapon under my command, a beast I tame with deft maneuvers. My hands dance on the wheel, a maestro conducting an orchestra of speed and steel and swerving, sliding, a delicate balance between control and chaos. Each turn, a potential kiss with calamity on this damn highway.

The night air rips through the open windows, tangling with my breath as I coax the car into a drift, tires screeching in protest. Death whispers, but I'm no easy mark. If it's my time, it is, but be fucking sure I'll haunt your perfect little ass until she's with me in hell, Fallon.

I haul on the handbrake, heart thundering, as I finally come to a stop. Sideways across the side of the road, my laughter fades into the stillness of the night. She tried to kill me and fuck, if that doesn't make me want her even more. My beautiful, deadly Fallon.

I step out of the car, hard asphalt beneath my feet. Looking down that endless road, I know there's no turning back. She's in my veins now, entwined in the chaos she conjures. Fucking twisted fates. Let's dance, bunny. Let's dance to the edge of the abyss and see who falls first. I'll fucking find you tonight.

I'm in Fallon's room, and she's not fucking there. My breath comes out in sharp, hot, and heavy bursts as the fury builds into a crescendo. After I stopped my car, I contacted Daniel to ask him to come get me. And when I asked if he had seen Fallon tonight, he said no. So, I assumed she was still in the house.

I storm through the corridor towards my control room, the air around me thick with the scent of my own anger, musky and intense. That little tease, always playing her daring games, sneaking around where she shouldn't be, it's fucking cute, or at least it used to be.

I scan the screen, my eyes searching for the one person that matters. I've been meticulous, obsessively so, deleting every piece of footage that even hints at her snooping, her defiance burning so bright. I'll be damned if Franco catches wind of her detective games, not on my watch. She's mine to deal with. Mine to protect.

The footage whirs to life, and there she is, trying her damnedest to dodge the cameras. She thinks she's being slick, but to me, she might as well be under a spotlight. Her movements are naïve, almost painfully so, and she's dressed like a goddamn hooker. My eyes devour the sight of her, even as the anger boils inside me. I need to find her. I need to drag her back and lock her away where the filth of this world can't touch her.

She's unaware of how much danger she's flirting with, and it's up to me to shield her from it and keep her safe from the chaos that threatens to engulf us both.

My attention is fixated on the screen as she slips into the night, my mind racing with the possibilities. Where are you, Fallon? And what the hell do you think you're doing out there? Because when I find her, all bets are off, and she'll learn just how far I'm willing to go to keep what's mine. Using my connections and stalker skills, I'm now, in the dead of night, in front of the *StarlightClub*. The pulsing beat of metal music reverberates through my chest as I push open the doors to the strip club. It's a nonsense of sounds and sights, repulsing me. Neon lights and glitters flicker in the air, casting a lurid glow across the amassed bodies.

The crowd is thick, a sea of lust. I wade through it, my eyes sharpening with intent. A group of men bellows like a pack of goddamn hyenas, their cheers spiking up over the music. They're focused on a single point, a stage where the main attraction unfolds, and like a motherfucker, it magnetizes my gaze.

She moves like sin on that stage, her body a tantalizing curve of motion. Half-naked, unapologetic, her breasts bare are perfect, and damn, I can't tear my eyes away. I'm entranced. Her movements sear into my brain, etching a permanent imprint.

I approach more, and the reality beneath the wig fucking drops a bomb. Fallon. My blood boils, a hot surge of anger and want consuming me. Every gyrating twist of her hips is a fucking call to my primal instincts.

I shove my way forward with a singular focus, elbowing through the bodies until I secure a spot at the front, directly in her line of sight. Her eyes find mine, a flicker of recognition sparking amidst her honey gaze, a silent challenge issued with a tilt of her head.

With every measured step, every undulating movement, she's speaking directly to me, and damn if my body doesn't respond with a hunger that's sharp and immediate. Desire coils within me, tightening its grip as she tosses her hair back, the black wig strands catching the light like fucking halo.

Fallon's body rolls and dips, her limbs moving with an intoxicating blend of innocence and depravity. The men around me fade into nothingness. It's just her and me, locked in a dance of silent communion where she strips away the layers, both fabric and metaphorical. But I'm going to have to gouge their eyeballs all out one day, thanks to that fucking goddess.

Her fingers skim along the supple contours of her flesh, teasing the fastenings of her lacy black underwear with a promise of more, each flick of her wrist sending a jolt straight to my cock. The music switches, and she moves with it. Demons by Plaza is playing, and I control myself, gripping the edges of my chair forcefully.

The way she bites her plump lower lip, it's like she knows exactly the sort of visions swirling in my head, the kind of raw, unchained activities I want to get up to with her. I almost feel the soft touch of her skin against mine. I visualize it, the sweet scent of her that I'm sure would drive me absolutely insane if I could lean in close enough to breathe her in.

The bass line pounds, echoing the rush of my pulse, and I find myself leaning forward, drawn irresistibly into her orbit.

My fists clenched, and my restraint tested to its fucking limits. She's a siren, and I'm a man willingly crashing upon her rocks. Time loses all meaning as she continues to tease and strip, her every action an erotic promise. She's got me hooked. And the infuriating part? She knows it. She knows she's got me by the balls, burning for her. Closing in, Fallon gets right up in my face, so close it's almost too demanding not to strangle her right now, and then, her tongue just skims my lips in this gutsy move. OK. This is a straight-up dare, shattering whatever willpower I had left. I'm moving before reason can take hold, pushing my chair to the floor. By the time I grab her, there's no semblance of control left, only the primal urge to claim, to take, to fucking own.

In one swift motion, I hoist her over my shoulder. Her body is firm and resistant against mine, her screams for help barely piercing the noise that envelops us.

Some guys make the mistake of approaching, thinking they can intervene, but they back off when they see it's me. They know better than to meddle in my affairs. The bartender yells out my name like a damn battle cry, solidifying the fear and respect I command in here.

Ignoring Fallon's struggles and the gasps around us, I stride out of the club. The cool night air hits me, but it's no match for the heat raging in me. As I carry her to my truck, the predator inside grins, relishing her fight. It's sick, it's wrong, but fuck if it doesn't turn me on even more.

The parking lot is practically deserted, the glow from the streetlight doing little to chase away the shadows. Her ass is up in the air, perfectly shaped, and just begging for attention. Without a second thought, my hand comes down hard, pinching her flesh with possessiveness. She's cursing and thrashing, but I'm beyond the point of hearing her protests. Throwing her into the trunk, I smiled at her before slamming the door in her face. Climbing into the driver's seat, I'm hit with Fallon's screams. "Let me out, you fucking psycho!" I laugh even harder. "Stop pretending your little show didn't fucking soak your panties little bunny. Now just fucking start yourself before we get home, and shut the fuck up."

CHAPTER 14

DANGEROUS GAME

FALLON

The world beyond the metal of the trunk fades to an echo as the engine's growling hum vibrates through my confined space. I'm curled, the chill of the truck floor seeping into my bones.

Camden's voice crackles through the small gap at the top of the back seat and where I am, distorted yet unmistakable. "I can't fucking wait," he breathes, a dark chuckle lacing his words. A twisted excitement shudders down my spine.

"Do you know what I'm doing?" His voice comes to me breathless, wild. "I'm jerking myself, baby. The sight of you, your perfect breast. Imagining tearing out the eyes of all those fuckers who have looked at what belongs to me. Fuck." He moans, and that's my undoing.

As the image of his muscular arm continues to dance through my thoughts, it feels like an intrusive guest, one I never invited but can't seem to banish. Every time I close my eyes, that rhythmic movement, full of strength and purpose, plays out like a forbidden movie. It's a scene that I didn't ask to witness, yet it captivates me in ways I can't explain.

My mind battles with these unwelcome feelings, trying to label them as mere fantasies or fleeting thoughts. But my body, a fucking traitor, betrays me. A surge of warmth radiates from deep within, settling in that intimate space between my thighs. It's an involuntary reaction that I neither anticipated nor wanted, yet it speaks volumes.

I find myself caught in this internal tug-of-war, wrestling with emotions and sensations that defy logic. How can something so forbidden feel so intensely exhilarating? The engine's hum is a distant drumbeat as his voice becomes the world. The desire in his tone is palpable. "You are the most perfect thing I ever laid eyes upon, bunny." He moans deeply, "Fuck baby, do you hear how hard I'm jerking myself?"

My flesh is sensitive to every jostle of the bump of the roads, every syllable he speaks, burning me more. My breath is ragged, the atmosphere charged with something animalistic and raw. My hands drift downward, seeking my own release, my touch igniting sparks that flicker through my veins. I slide two fingers along my wet folds, closing my eyes and imagining they are Camden's.

The truck moves at a steady pace that complements the rhythm of my fingers, delving deeper into my own wetness, stoking the fire that he has so deliberately lit. The crude sounds from both ends of the vehicle blend into a cacophony of debasement, yet I cannot halt the tide.

As my climax gets closer and closer, I'm unable to control my growing moans. "Are you touching yourself, Fallon? " He asks furiously. My only response is an even louder moan.

God, this is so fucked up. I'm breathing hard and fast when, without warning, the world tilts on its axis. The truck swerves like it's possessed, throwing me against the walls. My head's pounding, and I'm sure I'll have the bruises to show for it. But the pain is nothing compared to the swell of emotions threatening to choke me, the fear, the anger, and yeah... the fucking throbbing need that's got no damn to be there.

I'm still reeling when the truck grinds to a halt. Silence. The heavy thud of Camden's boots outside catches my attention. The doors open, and I'm blinded by the harsh streetlight that floods in, leaving me squinting, trying to adjust. Before I can even draw a sharp breath, one of Camden's large, rough hands wraps around my throat. He's choking the life out of me, squeezing tight as his other hand moves furiously over his hard, naked arousal.

"Fuck Fallon. Now. Be my good fucking girl, and watch me come for you." My eyes water both from the lack of oxygen and the way I love this scene in front of me. He's so big, fucking long and thick.

My survival instincts kick in hard, I'm scratching, kicking, trying to pry his fingers from my neck as his grip tightens, but he's like a goddamn vise. The strength in his hand is overwhelming, and I can feel the spots starting to float across my vision. But, even in my panic, I sense my evil pussy clench my orgasm.

It's fucking perverse watching him stroke himself with such vigor. As the tension in his body hits a fever pitch, he lets out a guttural sound, half-moan, half-growl, and comes with a shudder, his release splattering hot and sticky across my face.

I gasp, the fight in me roaring stronger. My lungs burn for air as his semen trickles down my skin, the salty, bitter scent invading my senses while I feel the last tremor of my own climax. Camden's grip on my throat finally loosens a cruel mercy allowing me to suck in greedy gasps of air. "Good girl, Fallon. "

I lay there, panting, covered in his release, my body responding in sickening ways to the horror of what's just happened. I'm a mess of emotions, the confusion and arousal mingling with a fucked-up kind of desire that makes me want to vomit. He's a psycho. And yet here I am, flushed, my body betraying me in the most primal of ways. Camden closes the door and steps away; I can only wait there, shaken and defiled, the twisted echo of my mind wanting more, the last thing I feel before the dark swallows me whole.

I awaken in stages, consciousness creeping up on me like the hesitant touch of the morning sun. My eyes flutter open, my vision blurred, my head pounding, a haze clouding the transition from dreams to reality. The air feels thick, my thoughts sluggish. I am adrift in a sea of warmth and comfort that feels both foreign and familiar. I glance down at my body. A large black T-shirt envelope my frame. It smells faintly of detergent and something else, a scent I can't quite place yet tugs insistently at the edge of my memory. The fabric is soft against my skin. My gaze wanders, the room coming into a gradual focus as I take in my surroundings. It's a room I've never seen before, but the arrangement feels intentional, lived-in. A pang of unease tightens in my gut. How did I get here?

My nose twitches, catching the traces of an aroma that niggles insistently at my senses. There is a hint of spice and wood, an olfactory echo that conjures the shadowy image of a man. Camden. The connection clicks, and a sliver of ice slides down my spine. He's not here, not within these four walls, but the imprint of his presence clings to the air like a whispered secret.

The realization hits me hard, the comfort of the bed suddenly feeling less like a sanctuary and more like a cage. I'm clean. Any trace of make-up from the night before has been erased, the wig that had been part of my disguise gone. And now that I remember, no trace of cum on my face. I'm stripped down to a self that feels too vulnerable, too exposed. My heart starts to race, thudding uncomfortably against the confines of my ribs. A million questions flit through my quickly clearing mind, each one a puzzle piece I can't quite place.

I swing my legs to the side of the bed, the cool air nipping at my exposed skin. A shiver runs through me, but it's not from the chill. I need answers, and the quiet of the room offers none. My fingers clench into the sheets, the cotton fibers twisting between my knuckles. I rise unsteadily, the room swaying slightly as I find my footing.

CHAPTER 15

SUBMISSION

FALLON

I emerge from Camden's room. The mansion looms around me, extravagant and silent. I'm in his part of the home. My bare feet padded softly against the cool, marbled floors.

I make my way along the corridor, the sound of the grand clock in the foyer tolling. As I glance over to the kitchen, I see him standing shirtless, his muscles defined and powerful. The light from the window highlights his toned physique, revealing scars that tell stories of his battles and challenges. Each scar emphasizes his strength, making him appear even more rugged and commanding. Witnessing such raw masculinity as he moves effortlessly, showcasing a blend of grace and power, is captivating.

But even if the sight of him makes me curious and aroused, it also fuels my anger. The vivid memory of being tossed into a trunk, exposed, and humiliated burns in my head. He had treated me like some kind of object and demeaned me in a way that ignited a vengeful fire in my chest. I can still feel his touch, still smell him on my skin, and I can't shake off the residue of his dominance. But at the same time, I believe I deserved it. After all, I did try to kill him. Part of me knew it wouldn't work. He's far too smart and trained. He knew what to do. And I even believe that a part of me wanted the punishment that would follow.

I catch sight of my reflection in the polished metal of the appliances, a flustered, furious mess. I snatch a knife from the counter. I brandish it at him, my hand steady despite the maelstrom of emotions in me.

"Camden," I hiss. My other hand trembles, not from fear but from the surging, overwhelming need to confront him.

He turns to face me and smiles at me with an almost childlike expression, a strange contrast to his rugged features, beard, and the few white hairs that shine in it. "I see you're waking up in shape, little bunny. " I want to slit his throat.

 "Do I need to remind you that you've tried, in vain, to kill me yesterday, Fallon? And when I found you, " his face is now enraged, furious as he advances towards the blade that I hold at arm's length. "You were dancing on a stage of a strip club, almost naked. Didn't you get the message with your date from the other day? You are mine."

With the blink of an eye, he twists my arms and rips the knife out of my hold. I grunt as I rub the spot where he made contact on my wrist. "YOU, son of a bitch!" I'm screaming louder than I'd like. I'm losing control. "I was almost there when you dragged your big ass in there!" I add. "What were you doing, Fallon?" His commanding voice, laced with concern and confusion, hardly rises above a whisper. However, its intensity cuts through the fog in my mind, causing me to recoil. I'm trapped, like a deer caught in headlights, paralysed, and unable to fucking move. I said too much. Damn.

"I was looking for information about your fucked up dad and the enterprise, ok? The manager offered me information if I made her money during the evening."

Camden's eyes darken as he slams one of the cabinet doors behind me, the sound echoing through the room and making me jump. The tension between us is a living thing, writhing and untamed. "I need to know," he growls, the words jagged and raw with a frustration that mirrors the chaotic rhythm of my own heartbeat. "What the hell will it take for you to stop this fucking investigation? What do you want?"

His question hangs in the air, laced with a desperation that's both captivating and terrifying. I can feel the anger emanating from him. "I don't play by your rules," I retort, my voice steady despite the quiver I feel in my limbs. I'm pushing back, daring him with something I know he can't resist.

He moves closer, the heat from his body a stark contrast to the cool air of the room. His eyes lock with mine, blue flames that sear through the shields I've meticulously built around myself. He's close enough for me to catch the faintest hint of mint from his breath, a small detail that inexplicably sends a shiver down my spine.

"Tell me what to do, Fallon," he demands, a dangerous edge to his voice that tells me he's walking a tightrope between control and chaos.

I sense his urgency, a dark and forceful wave threatening to pull me under. His nearness was intoxicating. His hands clenched at his sides, strong and capable, yet I see them tremble with the effort to restrain himself, not to touch, not take.

"Beg on your knees," I whisper. Heat flushes my cheeks as Camden's towering form lowers before me. His knees kiss the ground, and the imagery of a knight yielding to his queen sears into my consciousness.

Seeing him like that messes with my head, especially when his shadow looms large and dark over my thoughts. Here he is, Camden Betto, the monster incarnates, shrinking down before me into a form that should seem less threatening, less monstrous. But he still seethes danger from every pore, even on his knees.

I steel myself against the shock, my breath hitching slightly. My thighs press instinctively together, a feeble attempt to suppress the growing ache the building needs that sears its way up from my core. "Why are you doing this, Camden?" I ask. "You're mine. And I need to protect you." The power I wield at this moment casts a devious pleasure in the knowledge that I'm the one in control.

My lips part, a slow, involuntary response to the tumultuous desire that courses through my veins. I watch, my swallowing hard, as he leans forward, his face inching closer to the warm space between my thighs, just in front of my panties. His words reach me, a gruff whisper muffled by his closeness. "I can smell how excited your twisted mind is. You're wet for being in control." The raw truth in his voice seeps into my skin, intoxicating me with its vile sweetness.

His breath caresses my flesh, a soft, hot breeze that teases and tempts. And without warning, he sinks his teeth into the tender skin of my naked inner thigh, his mouth enveloping me in a feral gesture of possession.

A gasp escapes me, the sensation of his bite a savage blend of pain and pleasure. His tongue flickers against my skin, lapping at the sharp sting he's left behind.

He pulls back, eyes locked on mine from below. "Do what you want with me," he proposes his voice both a dare and a concession. "But remember, it'll come back around someday little bunny." He wants to prove his submission, to show that he's entirely within my grasp. He wants me to trust him. The significance of that isn't lost on me.

I bite my lower lip hard, savouring the metallic tang that fills my mouth as I consider his words. The idea of doing as I please to him, of using him in whatever way my depraved desires dictate, sends a shudder of arousal down my spine. But there's a warning there, a reminder that the tables can turn, that the hunter can become hunted. "Prove it," I murmur, the words tumbling from my lips like a dark incantation.

My hands find his hair, fingers tangling in the strands as I draw him closer to my pussy. "Show me how far you're willing to go to be at my mercy." Camden's response is immediate and savage, a testament to his resolve. He takes in his mouth almost all of my crotch, hot air on my intimate area, wetness envelops me, and I moan.

CHAPTER 16

UNTHINKABLE SACRIFICE

CAMDEN

My beautiful, deranged bunny pulls back, and I look into her eyes. Unfastening my pants button and pulling it down to my knees, I grab and start pumping my dick. I blow out my mouth, big breaths, and primal grunts of satisfaction as her hand suddenly connects to my fucking cheek. "Stop it, Camden. I didn't give you permission to touch yourself. "

I'm on the floor, the burn of that slap stinging across my face, but damn if it doesn't make me harder. Fallon's eyes are sparks of fire above me, looking down like she owns the place, and for a second, I almost let her believe she does. She thinks she's got the upper hand, that she's got me on my knees, but she's playing with fire, and she doesn't seem to comprehend it, even with my warning of retribution to come later.

My body's tight, so fucking hard it hurts, and it's all because of her. I'm wound up, ready to burst, and it's taking all I've got not to rip the little clothes on her. She needs the control. So, I'll let her have it for now.

"Get on all fours, Camden, like a good pup." She demands. The fucking balls this woman got. As I drop my hands to the floor, the cold tiles press against my palms and knees, sending a shiver through my body that has nothing to do with cold and everything to do with this sheer, perverse delight.

The ache in my groin is unbearable, a constant, throbbing pulse that's got my whole body vibrating like a strung-out guitar string. I'm watching her, daring her with my eyes to step closer, to cross that line, while every primal part of me prays she does. I want to feel her touch again, even if it's just another hit because, with Fallon, even pain feels like a goddamn caress.

And there it is, that sharp sting, another slap across my face, pushing me to the edge. The pain's a jolt, awakening every damn sense and making my skin buzz. It's fucked up, but it's a thrill like no other, and I'm drunk on it, on her, on this insane power she has over me that I've never let anyone have before.

She thinks she's breaking me, training me, but Fallon's got it all wrong. I'm not the one being tamed here. I'm the danger, the one she should be running from, and yet here we are, both caught in a game that's spiraling out of control.

She places her bare foot on my face, toes in my eyes and all. I move my face quickly and grab her arch directly between my teeth. She's got me on my knees now, but payback's going to be a bitch, and Fallon's going to learn that the hard way. "I want to touch you." Her voice is almost a murmur but, at the same time, full of curiosity. "I'm all yours, bunny. Do whatever you want to my damn body. I don't care. Bleed it, kill it, but touch me."

She looks at me for a long time, something new in her eyes—maybe surprise or disgust. I honestly don't give a shit. Fallon tells me to wait, not to move, and walks away. I hear the door closing, separating my house from my father's side.

I don't look up when she finally returns after what seemed like an eternity. I continue to stare at the floor, hard and impatient. Leaving her in control to tell me what to do is a new kind of drug. But I saw the pink dildo in her hand while passing to my right, dangling from her little hand. "Now Camden. Do you want to use a safe word?"

"No," my voice is confident. She's behind me. My little bunny turned into the evil snake, ready to crush his prey. And I'm here for it. Her soft hands rest on the back of my neck. They slowly slide down my spine, running down my skin in big zigzags that leave a trail of heat on me. "Grab your butt and spread your cheeks, Camden." Fuck, that authoritative voice creates spasms in my dick already on the verge of explosion. I take my butt with each hand and spread it apart until I feel the fresh air of the room directly on my asshole. "You want to fuck me bunny?" I ask.

She spits, a warm splatter on my ass that shocks me out of my temporary daze. But make some pre-cum drip from my tip. Fallon's hands are on me now, rubbing the spit into my skin, sending shivers up my spine and nape.

The slickness allows the dildo she's holding to glide around, teasing me and promising so much more. She's the psycho; she's my menace. "Can I touch myself, Fallon?" The words scrape out of my throat. "Yes," she growls. I reach down, my hand wrapping around my hard cock, the thrill of obedience mixing with the ache for release. She breaches me then, pushing inside, and it's a searing heat that spreads through my entire body. I buck against her rhythmically, her movements dictating my pace as I stroke myself in time. That's fucking heaven. I've never been penetrated before, but I'll probably do it again, but only by her. The slide of the dildo inside me and the drag of my hand on my own flesh builds an intensity that can only end one way. Sounds spill from me, grunts and low gasps that bounce off the walls and fill the room with the raw evidence of my need. The pain I feel keeps me sharp and turned on. Fallon is relentless, her pace unyielding, moaning while fucking me, and I'm so close, teetering on the brink. This isn't just pleasure; it's territorial, it's consuming, it's Fallon marking me as hers like I'll mark her mine.

And then, it crashes over me, a tidal wave of sensation that leaves me breathless and quaking. I come hard, spilling onto the floor. My moan echoes around us, a litany of release and surrender that serves as a testament to the power Fallon holds over me. Collapsing onto the floor, the fucking rubber dick bounces, and it makes me realize that Fallon dropped it. She's fucked me apart, and I've never felt more owned—or more accessible. Ready for what she wants from me next.

CHAPTER 17

BLOOD AND CLIMAX

FALLON

The lingering remnants of a self-satisfied grin still clinging to my lips. My gaze, heavy with intent and a feral kind of delight, zones in on the still-glistening dildo that's rolled to a halt.

Without hesitation, I move towards Camden's face with an animalistic grace, my hips swaying to the rhythm of my racing pulse. The distance between us disappears under the weight of my lust-fuelled determination. I stop before him, close enough to feel the heat radiating from his beautiful, firm skin. A slow, purposeful reach out, and my fingers, light as a whisper, capture the angular contour of his hairy chin. The barest pressure and I guide his face towards mine, our breaths mingling, a soft collision of anticipation and wild recklessness. His stubble prickles against the soft pads of my digits, sending a jolt through me. The air is thick with a voracious yearning that seeps into my every pore, encouraging me as our gazes lock in silent communion. It's an unspoken conversation, one fuelled by desire. As our eyes meet, an electric current ignites a fire in my core's depths. I can see the reaction in his eyes, blue like a winter storm, darkening with the same need that consumes me. This moment, charged with the explosive potential of our combined cravings, teeters on the edge of reason and madness.

My hands tremble with the urge to explore, to claim, to possess every inch of the enigma that stands before me, his psyche as exposed and vulnerable as his flesh beneath my grip. This is the precipice of our self-made abyss, where the line between control and chaos blurs into nothingness. Feeling pumped up like I'm about to chase something exciting, and with a buzz to conquer, I'm all set to dive deep into this craving, tempted by every little sign from Camden's breath. Leaning in closer, my voice lilts, low and sultry, "Am I as fucked up as you, Camden?" The question hangs in the air. I release my hold on him, stepping back just enough to stoke the flames of want that glimmer in his eyes. "Oh, bunny. I think you already know the answer." I explode. I can't contain it anymore.

I jump to my feet, tearing off my panties and my shirt, leaving me completely bare and, somehow, powerful. Camden's eyes burn a trail over my skin. He's naked, too, and I can't tear my eyes off his already new erection, hard and unyielding. It's there, proudly on display, stirring something wild within me. "Catch me, I want you to chase me." I challenge him, my voice a siren's call.

And like a force of nature, Camden rises, pure, unadulterated power in human form. The air between us crackles with electricity, each breath charged with anticipation. With a predatory grace, he closes the distance. His intent laser-focused on me. His movements are decisive, a hunter's precision that knows no hesitation. "Bunny, I knew that your desires were as dark as mine. You fucking goddess. I'll chase you if that's what you want." I stand before him, my heart hammering in my chest like a drumbeat to this carnal dance. There's no turning back now. The game has changed, but I'm ready. There's no hiding the hunger in his eyes, no mistaking the carnal intent behind his gaze. It's raw, visceral, and promises a union of bodies that will write its own primal story. I'm ready for him, ready for the storm. And as he approaches even more, I brace for the impact of the inevitable collision. "Now run."

Panic claws at my insides as I sprint towards the kitchen island, my bare feet slapping the cold tile. My breath comes in ragged heaves, my heart a fierce drum in my chest, pounding a rhythm of sheer adrenaline and fear. I'm feeling that gut-wrenching fear like I've never felt before; at this moment, Camden's the hunter, and I'm definitely the hunted. All I'm thinking about is getting to that island, hoping it'll keep us apart. Camden's dark and menacing laughter chases me just as fast as his footsteps. It echoes around the kitchen, a haunting soundtrack that sends shivers down my spine. I glance back just in time to see him round the corner of the counter, his hand snatching a steel blade from the block. Oh God. His laughter intensifies, growing wild and untamed, bouncing off the walls and curdling the blood in my veins. I push harder, my legs aching as I launch into a full sprint down the corridor that seems to stretch into infinity, Camden's presence looming ever closer. The house's acoustics magnify every sound. Every muscle in my body kicks into gear. It's as if instinct takes over, pushing aside all other distractions or thoughts. The increasing intensity of Camden's footsteps echoing behind me are a stark and chilling reminder of my predicament. Each step he takes amplifies the reality sinking in. I'm not just being pursued physically, but in that raw, elemental sense where survival becomes the only game in play. I fucking regret asking for this. Because even if it's what I wanted and asked for, I now fear for my fucking life.

I flee down the never-ending corridor, naked and exposed, with my stepbrother now close enough to reach out and seize me. Standing in front of a closed door. My hands are shaky as I twist the doorknob rapidly, my breath hitching when it refuses to budge. Locked. Fuck. A surge of panic rises in my chest, my pulse racing. Suddenly, the cold kiss of steel just under my earlobe has me frozen in place, every muscle coiled tight. There's a whisper of movement, a shadow sliding closer, and Camden's mouth is against my neck, his breath hot on my skin. I shiver, caught between fear and a dark, twisting heat that blooms inside me despite the danger. A moan escapes my lips while closing my eyes. "You trying to escape me, Fallon?" His voice is a low growl, a velvet threat that wraps around me. It's filthy and rough, the undercurrent of lust unmistakable. "You should know by now that I'm the only way out." His tongue flicks out, tracing the same path of the knife's point in a way that's so wrong, but my body betrays me, responding with an involuntary arch towards him. God, this is insane. "Didn't your mama ever warn you about playing with fire?" he teases, his breath warm against my skin, his knife still threatening a deadly dance along my neck. "Now, bunny. I'll tell you once. If you want me to stop, I will do it anytime. But you have to say the word forgiving." His mouth closes over my ear again, this time biting until the pinch is almost unbearable. "But if you cry, scream, say no or stop, I'll go on mercilessly."

I nod silently, swallowing hard, and without wasting a second, he turns me around and places me on his shoulder. A hard slap hit my ass, and I hiss in pain. He walks briskly and enters his room before throwing me onto the bed like a rag doll. I feel the weight of his body as he crashes down over me, the bed dipping under our combined mass. The air is thick with the musk of his skin and the faint tang of metal as the knife hovers between us, a lethal promise, a tool of control poised with the precision of a practiced hand. My pulse hammers in my throat, a frantic rhythm that sings a dangerous duet with the erratic beat of Camden's heart against my ribcage.

The cool edge of the blade rests against my chest, a hair's breadth from piercing skin, from drawing forth the lifeblood that thrums beneath. His eyes, heavy with dark desire, meet mine. They're like twin voids, all-consuming, threatening to swallow me whole. His gaze commands my submission, and my body betrays me again, responding with a tremble, a silent plea for something I can't quite name. "You're going to have to tell me who left you with that scar so I can go rip out his heart." He looked pissed.

I become self-conscious for a few moments, realizing that naked, lying on my back, in the light, we can see the scar between my breasts. But before I have time to think about it too much, his mouth is on me, biting one of my nipples. I arch my back with a groan. The air's thick with our energy, a wild vibe making it tough to even think straight. Every part of me feels alive like I'm on the edge of losing it. I'm all caught up in this intense pull from Camden, in this crazy, deep need that's hard to shake off. Everything's so charged up like we're in our own world where nothing else matters. And in that crazy moment, I'm just totally hooked, pulled in by him. The twisted pleasure-pain that threatens to consume us both. The room spins, and I'm falling, spiraling down into an abyss that promises ecstasy and oblivion in equal measure.

"Who hurt you?" He asks again. But I don't answer. I buck my hip, grinding slowly on his rock-hard dick. I feel the blade tracing a teasing path along the tender expanse of my inner thigh. "Stay still, Fallon," Camden's breath washes over my skin, laced with a threat that sets my heart racing. The metallic tang of my own blood reaches my nostrils as the cut opens, a bead of crimson blossoming under Camden's meticulous guidance.

His tongue flicks out, lapping at the fresh wound, and I suppress a moan. The heat of his mouth against my flesh sends a shockwave of pleasure that shouldn't be there. His eyes meet mine, sharing a look that's all fire and sin as he paints stripes of my blood all over my skin. It's so wrong it's right. His fingers are rough and demanding, smearing the red liquid like a forbidden ointment across my pussy. "You're so beautiful when you're dirty," he whispers huskily, turning my blood into an unholy lube.

The scent of iron and arousal hangs heavy between us, and I feel the slickness of my own desire pooling between my legs, spreading on his fingers. I'm so fucking turned on. It's unreal. Camden's eyes gleam with satisfaction. "You're mine." He says. I'm lost in his words, lost to him. The raw surge of heat envelops me as his fingers slip inside me, an invasion that draws a gasp from my throat. His digits drive deep, relentless in their pursuit of my pleasure. Curling up to press on the right spot. The walls of the room fade away, and the world narrows down to the feel of him. Heat pools in my belly, my limbs tremble, and my moans fill the chamber, uninhibited, a symphony of delight. Camden's mouth claims mine with equal fervor, his tongue repeating the same violent dance as his fingers. Every push, every twist sends me spiraling closer to the edge.

The intensity grows, a crescendo of sensation, as he alternates between forceful thrusts and teasing licks. Knowing that my juice and blood are mixing, using it as a lubricant makes me roll my eyes to the back of my head with pleasure. The earlier pain from the cuts now forgotten. His breath is hot, his bites bordering painfully good on my flesh.

"Dirty little thing," he growls, the vibrations of his voice sending ripples through me. "Beg for it." The world spins, and I'm teetering on the brink of oblivion. His words are filthy poetry, stoking the flames that threaten to consume me whole. A part of me should recoil, but the truth is, I crave this madness, this reckless abandon. He put his face between my legs, looking me in the eyes as he hovers over my bloody pussy. He bites down on my swollen nub, the pain sharp and exquisite. It's the final trigger.

My body convulses, a starburst of pleasure that obliterates reason, and my orgasm crashes over me with the force of a tidal wave as he sucks on it. Camden's fingers don't relent, drawing out my pleasure until I'm nothing but a quivering mass of nerve endings—Spent, his name a whispered benediction on my lips. My vision darkens, and the exhaustion carries me away.

CHAPTER 18

TROUBLED PAST

FALLON

The soft caresses of Camden's hands across my skin feel surreal, his unexpected gentleness a stark contrast to the heat of his gaze. I'm lying in his bed, trying to make sense of the delicate touch that somehow seems both familiar and shocking. It's like he's tracing secrets on my flesh or trying to heal the mark he left yesterday. I'm still reeling from our little chase. The memory of his mouth on me still burns. His tongue dancing across places I never knew could hold such fire, awakening a hunger

I'm almost scared to acknowledge. I remember slipping into sleep afterward, spent and sated in a way I've never been. Yes, I've slept with guys and had oral sex with them, too. But never have I had this kind of sex. And I'm afraid it will be the only way for me in the future. And now, in the quiet aftermath of passion, I'm cocooned in sheets that smell like him. His blue eyes, those pools of mystery and darkness, watch me as I stir, and I can't help the flush that heats my cheeks. I'm naked under his gaze, literally and metaphorically, the vulnerability almost too much to bear. His voice breaks the silence, a low murmur that vibrates through the air. "What's this scar from Fallon?" I hesitate, unsure how much I'm ready to reveal, but the tenderness in his eyes encourages me. It's a strange moment of intimacy in a world of harsh reality. "I don't have many memories of my childhood. Sometimes, I still have strange reactions and little flashbacks, but nothing concrete." I lay on my side to face him. "Valentina told me that I got sick when I was very young because of mold in our beat-up apartment. The doctors had to clean and drain my lungs." It's as if our very souls are bared in this quiet space, and I can't shake the feeling that something has shifted between us, something profound. I've never felt so exposed yet so strangely safe. "I'm sorry, bunny. You want me to burn down the hospital to the ground?" I laugh. A sincere one and it seems to shock him to the core. His hands find my face, and I lean into it, closing my eyes. "You're the greatest threat I've ever seen in my life, Fallon. I've tried to push you away. But you're fucking hard head didn't catch up as I had planned." I sigh and laugh softly. "And what about your scar Camden?"

His face hardens, and I can see in his eyes the tsunami of emotions coursing through him. Perhaps he's not as psycho as I thought. Or I am more than I imagined. There's a shift in the air, the bed dips, and Camden pulls himself out of our tangled warmth. He slips into his boxers, simple, black, clinging to him, and he's up, feet hitting the floor.

The sight of him, muscles flexing beneath his skin, the play of shadow and light dancing over his back, it's a distraction. His face twisted up with all the shit he tries to keep locked down, tells the tale of the hurt he's nursing. And it hurts me. He roams the room, trapped in his own personal hell, and I can see it, the crack in his armor, the way he clenches his fists. "He treated me like shit. Like I was just a piece of trash he couldn't be bothered to toss out," he spits out, each word soaking in a venom that's aimed at a ghost. Anger got him shackled, got his jaw set hard, and I can hear the soft grind of teeth as he holds back the urge to smash something. And it's not just anger. It's something wounded, some raw piece of him cracked wide open with the telling. The silence folds around us, heavy like a thick blanket, stifling and suffocating. The ghosts from his past are here now, hovering in the dim light, and I feel them, too, those remnants of pain and neglect that shaped Camden into the man he is. He stops, turns to me, and it's all right there, his torment, like a physical thing, like I could reach out and touch it. "He'd hit me, didn't feed me, neglect me. No reason, no fucking rhyme to it, just because he could." His voice cracks, a sound so brittle it could shatter glass. "He used me like a lab rat. And I've got the marks that remind me of it every fucking day."

I'm silent, letting his words hang, fighting my tears. Camden's wounds are deep, carved by a lifetime of being treated like he didn't matter, like he didn't deserve nothing, like a monster. "Fallon. You need to understand that Franco is dangerous. The enterprise is dangerous. Hell, I'm dangerous. I'm never going to let you go now. And that makes me fucking angry. Because you're in danger." I get up and join him without bothering to cover my naked body. With him, I don't feel the need. I grab his face between my two hands and force him to stop moving. "I wouldn't want to be anywhere else but here." He stares at me, and his face tilts to the side as if he is looking at a strange animal. "Bunny. I'm not a nice guy hiding under a bad one. I'm a monster with a conscience, but a monster." I close my eyes for a few seconds and smile at him. He smiled at me, a genuine smile with a hint of malice. "Fuck baby, if I didn't have so much to explain to you right now, I'd pick you up and fuck your asshole until you lose consciousness." I'm perched on the kitchen island's edge, nursing my steaming cup of coffee like it's my lifeline. The rich, dark aroma intertwines with the crisp scent of bacon and eggs that sizzle in the pans Camden masterfully handles. His back to me, he moves with the certainty of a chef, flipping bacon with an almost elegant flick of his wrist. Each crackle and pop from the skillet is a culinary symphony, a background track to the bombshell he's casually dropping on me like it's everyday chit-chat. "So, let me lay it out straight for you, bunny," He speaks, his voice a smooth purr that somehow makes the horror of his words sting even more. "The family business... we pluck people from their pretty little lives, drag them out to the middle of Death Valley, and our doctor harvests their organs." He flips an egg, catching it effortlessly. "And then sell the parts to the highest bidder." I grimace, swallowing a mouthful of coffee that suddenly tastes bitter. The reality he paints is gruesome, yet there's an artful nonchalance in the way he moves around the room as if he's discussing stock investments rather than human lives. "And that's not all," he continues, sliding the cooked bacon onto a paper towel to drain. "We get orders in containers filled with human cargo." Camden's demeanor doesn't falter, his eyes focused on the task at hand.

I blink, trying to process the information, the weight of his words settling in my stomach like lead. Around us, the kitchen feels too bright, too ordinary for such a conversation. The golden hue of the morning sun streaming through the windows seems at odds with the darkness he's unveiling. The eggs sizzle, a gentle reminder of the rapidly slipping normalcy. A soft clink of cutlery against the plate as he serves up the breakfast he's prepared. There's a twisted sense of domesticity in the air, made all the more surreal by the fact that I'm sharing this moment with the man who's just shattered any semblance of innocence this day held. My grip tightens around the mug, the heat searing into my palms, but it's nothing compared to the heat of the revelation burning through my mind. What kind of a family have I gotten myself tangled up with? And more importantly, how the hell am I supposed to sit here, sipping my coffee, while Camden lays out his soulless routine like he's discussing the weather? "We have teams here that kidnap adults all over the casinos, bars any place owned by Betto company. But containers are mostly children. Which come from other countries." A part of me wants to bolt, to scream, to run, to reject this grotesque reality, but I'm frozen, caught in the web of Camden's dark world. And despite it all, despite the revulsion clashing violently with the tantalizing danger he embodies, I can't ignore the undeniable pull toward the abyss he's offering me a glimpse into. I want to throw up. I want to do something.

"And you're ok with that? You... You participate in this." I ask. I can't keep my tears inside and I burst into tears.

CHAPTER 19

TO BURN AN EMPIRE

FALLON

I can't believe this shit. Standing there with tears streaming down my face after Camden drops that fucking bomb on me. He closes the gap between us fast as hell, and before I know it, his arms are around me, crushing me in a vice grip.

I'm flailing for a second, trying to shove him off because nobody gets to manhandle me like this. But he doesn't budge. Holds me tighter like he's trying to solder his strength into me or something.

After I struggle like a cornered animal, I finally go still, sagging against his chest. Camden sighs like he's got the weight of the fucking world on his shoulders. "No, Fallon, I'm not okay with this." The rawness in his voice is so out of left field that I can feel it vibrating through me. "Killing's a part of me, yeah," he goes on, "but I only get off on it when there's a damn good reason. Innocents? Kids? That shit doesn't deserve a toast."

"For years, I've been grinding, hustling day in and day out, trying to earn even just a sliver of trust from my old man. You know how it is in this family business. Every move, every decision, it's all under his watchful eye. Climbing those ranks wasn't about the title or the recognition; it was about proving to him that I could make something of myself in his world. But listen closely, little bunny, because here's the kicker. All this time, while he's been patting me on the back, I've been plotting. Fuck, you heard me right. Every nod of approval it's been leading to this moment. I've been biding my time, setting the stage, and I'm damn well ready to flip that script on him. He won't see it coming, and when it happens, he'll realize just how wrong he was about me. So buckle up because things are about to get interesting, and dear old dad won't know what hit him."

I'm still hanging onto him, my head spinning with everything he's telling me. It's like I'm trying to process one bomb after another. It's fucking chaos in my head. I'm pissed off, twisted up, but somehow, his confession it's grounding me too. Makes me see he's not just a cold-blooded killer, even if that's what he thinks. He's got layers, and they're as complicated as a maze.

His heart's pounding against my ear, so damn loud it's like it's drilling the truth into me. Camden's playing a risky as-hell game, but he's doing it for reasons that aren't just about power or money. It's about flipping the whole fucked-up world on its head.

And it makes me feel something weird in my gut. Respect, or maybe it's something more dangerous. God help me because whatever's happening here is way out of my playbook. I'm in some deep, dark water with Camden. "I wanna help," I blurt out, my words hanging in the air, heavy and uncertain. It's like dropping a match in dry grass, the way his anger flares. "Nope. No, Fallon."

I don't do well with being told what to do. I never have. The itch to push back and argue is fierce in my belly. But I don't want to fight. Not now. Not over this. So, I bite down hard on my tongue, tasting blood, and let the moment pass. "I need to go back to the other side of the manor, Camden. Can't risk Franco and Valentina getting suspicious if they don't see me for meals." I lay it out plain and simple, with no room for argument. Camden's face is still all hard lines and shadowed eyes, but I don't stay to see if he'll soften. I jump down from the kitchen island and turn on my heel, heart hammering like it's trying to break out of my chest. As I walk away, it feels like I'm leaving something unfinished, something important. But what choice do I have? I can't let Franco and Valentina start asking questions; I can't give them a reason to poke their noses into my business. And I won't argue with him about my participation.

With each step I take, the urge to look back gnaws at me. I don't, though. I keep moving, thinking only of the cool darkness on the other side of the manor, where I can breathe, where I can plot, where I can figure out my next move without him breathing down my neck. But even if I don't look back, that doesn't mean I don't feel his eyes on me, burning a hole into my head as I walk away.

Franco's eyes have been following me like a hawk everywhere I go, and it's been two long days since Camden spilled his guts about the brutal truths hidden behind the gloss of the Betto empire. The organ trafficking is the real deal.

I haven't seen him nor heard from him since, and truth be told, I haven't been looking. My mind's been wrestling with the gravity of it all. I needed that space to let the horror settle, to comprehend the monstrous reality I'd stumbled into.

But now, I can't shake off the weight of Franco's gaze. His eyes are on me, probing, dissecting my every move. It's like he's waiting, biding his time to corner me with questions.

I sit at the breakfast table, the clink of my fork on the plate and the delicate aroma of freshly brewed coffee doing nothing to ease the tension knotted in my core. Valentina's laugh rings out, a jingling accompaniment to Franco's steady fingers drumming on the table. It's like a performance, a rehearsed play of normalcy, but each of us wears a mask.

I push the food around on my plate, the taste like ash in my mouth. I can't eat with the sour tang of dread coating my tongue. I glance up, and Franco's eyes meet mine. The air thickens, choking me with the unsaid.

Across the table, Valentina's smiling like she's never been that happy, her movements punctuated by the tinkling charm of her bracelet, a sound that used to be comforting but now feels hollow. I have to keep up the act, smile politely, and nod at the appropriate moments. "Franco, I wanted to post on social media today, and I was wondering if you have anything in particular that you'd like me to share." He smiles at me, and my stomach rolls. "We will start raising funds for our charity, which provides medical equipment in Asia; the event will be a masquerade ball in a month."

He shoves a piece of sausage into his mouth. "Is that enough to keep you busy, Fallon? " Inside, I'm a roiling storm, a chaos waiting to unfurl. It's a delicate balancing act, keeping the facade intact while my insides churn with the knowledge of the darkness that plagues within these walls. Camden's confessions bind us together in this hellish tapestry. He wants to protect me. But he is part of the danger. I nod and continue to eat my fruit.

I've spent the day alongside Valentina, drifting through stores, filling the void with material things and conversations as empty as the smiles we offered one another. Surrounded by the stillness of my room, shadowed and serene, I lay sprawled across my bed, my gaze fixed on the laptop's glow. The soft hum of its machinery is a whisper against the silence enveloping the space. Each click and each scroll is robotic. I'm sifting through the facets of my online persona, steeped in superficial glitz that masks the turmoil within. My mind is a warren of thoughts, each turning over the same futile question: how can I help?

The night grows dense around me. It's late, and the world outside my window is a dark abyss, the perfect mirror for the sense of futility that grips me. The task at hand, the content meant for posts and messages, seems trivial against the backdrop of my gnawing contemplation. The social media management of the Betto enterprise feels like chains, binding me to a virtual performance when the real act is playing out behind closed doors.

With each tap on the keyboard, the reality of my dilemma weighs heavier on my shoulders. The magnitude of this empire of blood, the strings that pull at the fabric of society, and the secretive snakes I'm surrounded by all make me feel minuscule, powerless. It's a game with stakes so high, and I'm unarmed.

I roll onto my stomach, elbows digging into the soft mattress, fingers pausing over the keys. The riddle of how to dismantle something so monolithic without being crushed under its collapse lingers on the fringes of my consciousness.

My chest rises and falls with the rhythm of my internal tumult, the scent of vanilla from my earlier shower mingling with the lavender air or my clean sheets. I can't stop thinking about Camden, too; I have so many questions, so many feelings, and so many things I want to talk about with him. But mainly, I'm wondering if we'll have a chance to be together, in a normal life one day.

CHAPTER 20

THE MASK

CAMDEN

I kick open the door to the house, and the stench of blood and grime clings to me like a second skin. My latest kill, one of the distributors, was just another stepping stone in my own clandestine crusade, a necessary bloodshed. I'm still riding that high, the raw, addictive rush of being the hunter, taking a life.

The first order of business is surveillance. I need to see her, to watch Fallon's through the unblinking eyes of the security cams. I make a beeline to the screens, the flickering of monitors a silent greeting. As I scan the footage, there she is my little bunny, sitting with Franco this morning, her innocent eyes wide but probing, a look I know too well. Franco's glance, fuck, the way that snake watches her when she's not paying attention, it's something feral, something that sets my blood ablaze with possessiveness. And not surprisingly, she's been prying, asking too many damn questions. Again.

She's mine, all spitfire and defiance wrapped in a package too fucking beautiful for this world. Watching her, seeing her interact with Franco, it's like a gut punch every damn time. My grip's vice-like on the mask in my hand, the skeleton mask still stained with the blood of the man I just cut into pieces, alive, little bit by bit.

I can't keep the growl from my throat, imagining that blood was spilled for her to keep her safe from the filth. I slip the mask on, its presence a familiar embrace, the adrenaline surging new life into my veins. I move, swift and silent, a specter drawn to her room. I need to remind her, to etch it into her fucking being, that her curiosity, her questions, they come with a price. In my world, you don't just ask. You learn to obey.

I stalk the corridors, a ghostly avenger with a burning need to dominate. As I draw closer to Fallon's room, my breaths are deep and even, the chill of the mask contrasting with the fire in my gut. She needs to be taught a lesson. One she won't forget anytime soon.

I burst into Fallon's room, my entrance a blend of force and precision that's got my blood pumping hard. She's there, startled from her relaxed position.

I can tell she doesn't know it's me beneath the skeleton's face, and the fear dancing in her eyes is intoxicating, fueling a deep excitement within me. Her panic, thick as the darkness we're enveloped in, scrambles her senses, making her hurl objects in blind terror.

Her desperation is a melody to my ears, and it sets my pulse throbbing in a dangerous rhythm. My dick is so hard it hurts. I stalk towards her, my blade an extension of my hand, glinting sinisterly in the meager light. With practiced swiftness, I grab her, my movements so fluid and assured that it's like we're in a dance designed by fate.

My arm snakes around her, the knife pressing close enough under her chin to promise danger without spilling her precious blood, yet.

I slap a hand over her mouth, the thrill of the hunt surging through me as I feel her pulse leap beneath my fingers. I can nearly taste her fear, and it's goddamn sublime. I press myself against her, my erection a solid line against her back. Her breaths come sharp and fast, fluttering against my hand. I peel my hand away from her mouth, keenly aware that even if she screams, no one will hear her. We're isolated in the depths of the house, far from the other bedrooms and common areas.

Her silence surprises me, a welcome twist in this little game. I let my gloved fingers dance along Fallon's neck, trailing down until they encounter the fabric of her little white tank top, no bra, how I like it.

I circle the stiff peak of her breast with a predator's precision, and a soft groan rumbles out of me as I pinch her nipple hard. Fallon's breath quickens, her body instinctively arching into the assault, puffing out her chest in response.

The heat in the room seems to spike, my mouth mere inches from her ear under the mask. It's a twisted kind of intimacy, one I savor in the darkest corners of my soul.

Fallon, my little bunny, her pulse races beneath the surface of her soft skin. I can feel it pounding. And as I grope her, claiming her with my touch, I know this is only the beginning of our twisted dance. Greedily, my hand finds the edge of her jogging pants, an intrusion, a claim. I press up against her, my arousal blatant. She's mine, a fact I sear into her with every rough rub of my body against hers.

With a surge of strength, I hurl her onto it and rapidly cage her with the weight of my body on hers. There's a madness here, a frenzy, as I pin her down, my intentions carved into the space between us.

The room falls silent as I stand above Fallon, the lone tear on her cheek a moment of vulnerability I capture in my mind like a photograph. My head tilts curiously as if I'm considering a strange new specimen that's come under my blade. The fear in her eyes is clear as she stares directly into my mask. My gloved hand steadies, the knife sharp and ready. With a single, smooth, almost graceful movement, I slice through her tank top, the fabric parting like a curtain. Her breasts bared to me, exposed and perfect, bouncing from her cries. I can't help the pleasure that rumbles deep within me. My breath hitches, hot and heavy, as I lean in, close enough for the blood of my last victim on the plastic of my mask to stain her face, a macabre kiss she can't avoid. There's poetry in this madness, an unspeakable art to the way she's laid bare and trembling under me. The worst part is that I know how much she loves it because I know her. Probably more than herself.

This is one of the advantages of having a sharp and deranged mind like mine. Calculating and cold, but clever at understanding others.

I'm fixated on her submission, the way she's splayed out and helpless, my dark desires unfolding before me. The glint of my blade returns to her throat while my other hand dives into her shorts beneath her panties.

My fingers close over her. She's drenched, and I groan, rolling my eyes, intoxicated by the confirmation of her arousal, the duality between her fear and her desire. Fallon's wetness is an unspoken plea, my grip on her, a full assertion of my control. I'm lost in the act, animal instinct overwhelming the remnants of any civilized restraint.

She moans and closes her eyes as I press the blade stronger against her skin, remove my hand from her pussy, and use it to gently pull up my mask while speaking to her in a deep voice. "Oh, bunny. Does daddy know you like to be chased away by your monstrous brother?" Her eyes immediately rounded, and her perfect lips parted a little.

She tries to move underneath me, but my blade presses so hard on her throat that the flesh almost cuts. "You fucking asshole. You scared me." She yells. "And you like that baby girl. I know it." I continue the movement to remove the mask completely when she raises a trembling hand, still in shock. "Keep it."

Smiling, I place it on my forehead. "Beg for it." I love her fucked up mind so much. Mine. "Please, Cam. Keep it." I think it's the first time I've seen so much vulnerability and embarrassment on her face when she looks at me. Her cheeks, now pink, my new favorite fucking color. A low growl laugh escapes me. "Do you want to play bunny?" She nods her chin very gently. The weight of my gaze pins her to the spot, my head tilting with a predator's interest. Fallon's tears carve a track down her cheek. I stand, shedding the gloves and putting them on the floor. With methodical precision, I reposition the bloodied mask upon my face, an action that speaks of ritual, of transformation, of a return to the persona that commands and terrifies. I retreat to the shadows like a spectre, my form melting into an oversized lecture chair in the corner of her room. My voice, a sultry tone that weaves through the room. "You dirty whore. You thought I was an intruder, and you were all fucking wet for him. Someone else." I shake my finger in a side-to-side motion. "You must be punished." The confusion and fear in her face war with the heat I know my voice ignites between her thighs. "Crawl to me, Fallon." I gently pat one of my knees.

"Now."   She quickly rises to my voice, which is now much louder and more authoritative. "Good girl." She gets on all fours, perfect breasts swaying from left to right as she approaches me gently without ever taking her eyes off my face. I'm so hard, my pants now rubbing against my painful erection. As she approaches, I untie the black jeans I'm wearing and grab my dick to pull it out, and a grunt of relief escapes me. I can see my little bunny licking her lips and almost drooling directly on the floor. "You want my dick to choke you, Fallon?" She sits still in front of me, ass on her heels. She nods and continues to stare at my cock. My hand is quick, and I slap her on one breast before sitting straight down again. "Look at my face, Fallon."

CHAPTER 21

DRUNK ON PAIN

FALLON

The pinch of the slap heats up the side of my boob. And I stare at him straight in the eye. I want to punch him in the balls for doing that to me. But at the same time, fuck I want it. In all my life, my desire has never been so high.

I am on the floor before a man, or rather, a god of death. That's a first. His mask, empty with emotion, stares at me. Topless, my panties soaked with pleasure. "Come lick your dick, Fallon." I wish I could take more time to assimilate what he has just said, but the need to touch him, to taste him, has been so strong that I lean hungrily towards his length.

I stick out the tip of my tongue and press it against the base of his large member, licking a path with minimal pressure to his head. A low growl escapes from the mask at the top of me, and I lay my eyes on him. I am opening my mouth as much as I am physically capable of and taking his head in my mouth, sucking.

A little moan echoes in my throat. "Fuck, good girl, Fallon. You take me so well in your mouth." With his encouragement, my arousal grows even more, and I continue to suck while bringing my other hand to my pussy, stroking her, the wetness giving me chills.

Pushing a finger into my wet slit, I feel my lips enveloping me, and I rub without mercy, the pleasure sending shocks all over my body. I increase the rhythm of the back and forth of my mouth on Camden when he grabs me by the hair at the nape of my neck rigorously, lifting my face, which releases his cock with a pop. "Such a good fucking girl for me. Look at you. With the blood of a dead man on your face, running a finger through your wet pussy."

I almost come right there, closing my eyes, the burning sensation on my scalp mixed with the pleasure between my legs and the words coming out of his mouth.

This motherfucker just grabs my hair even more strongly, and I hiss in pain. "Now, bunny. Come sit on your snake's dick like the good girl I know you are." I'm questioning the sanity of myself because this moment seems like a damn fever dream. The good, the bad, everything seems so confusing right now to me.

I get up quietly at my full height and approach Cam. His eyes burning with passion, desire and visibly impatience. I move forward cautiously and place myself directly on his thighs, my only protection, my soaked panties.

As soon as I sit entirely on top of him, he repositions himself so that his hard dick is directly on my cunt, and I roll my eyes, almost delirious, as the sensation of his rough grinding against my center is pushing me to the edge of orgasm. "Ah fuck Fallon." He wispers.

Without having full control of my own body, I start rocking against him, gripping both of his shoulders. I bring my face close to his mask, covered in blood and lick it with the tip of my tongue. The metallic taste fills my mouth, and I can't help but feel a shiver of warmth coursing through me. "So dangerous, my little bunny." He laughs.

His strong hands grab my panties on the front just above my pubic area, and with a single movement, he tears them, making me let out a cry. "Do you want me to keep my mask on to fill your wet cunt?"

I nod, the words stuck in my throat. And he laughs, a deep laugh that seems to come from the back of his throat. One of his hands goes back to one of his jeans pockets, and he pulls the knife out.

My heart beats faster in my chest. I prepare myself for the impact of the blade against my skin, and he holds it to me by holding it from the cutting side, giving me the handle. "Do whatever you wish with my body. It's yours." He speaks. In this moment, I decide to let myself fully into my desires and firmly take the handle between my fingers. Without wasting a second, I return the earlier favor and place the knife directly on his neck, under his chin, and the fucker moans. Fuck, the sound. "You think you're a snake, Cam? No. You're my sweet little dog." I say sensually.

He stills for a few seconds before lifting a hand and grabbing the blade, but not taking it out my hold. Inquietude grows in me as I look at it and start to feel him putting more and more pressure on his own skin until I see blood flowing and falling on my thigh. Taking a deep breath without moving or hesitating, I don't move. He's testing me. He wants to see if I'm going to back off. "Bleed for me, Camden," I add.

He taps my hand, sending the blade flying across the room, and violently grabs one of my breasts in his palm, squeezing and massaging it. Seized by a passion as strong as a storm, I spit directly on his cock, lift myself up and place the entrance of my pussy with the head of his length.

Pushing myself inch by inch, I close my eyes; everything is stimulating, almost too much, the smell of his perfume, the scent of my arousal, the sounds and moans he makes every time I impale myself a little more. The pain of the act is the only thing that still keeps me grounded in this moment.

I'm crying, almost halfway down on him. I stop moving. "I can't take it anymore. It's way too big." He puts both his hands on my shoulders and pushes me down, hard but slowly; using his hips too, he pushes them upwards, and I'm submerged with the intensity. I bite my lip with the sensation of pain burning in my core, tears starting to rise in the corner of my eyes. "Shhh... just a little bit more." He whispers mockingly in my ears.

With his words, he gives a sharp push that makes his entire cock enter me. A scream escapes my mouth, and he laughs, remaining motionless inside me to give my body time to adjust. Still a little shocked by the intrusion but much more comfortable, I open my eyes to find myself face-to-face with the black void of eyes in front of me.

Grabbing me by the legs, he lifts himself off the chair and carries me to the bed, never separating the connection that unites us. "Fuck Fallon. I've been dreaming of this moment. Do you remember your safe word?" I nod. He starts to move back and forth inside me, and the feeling is so good; I put my hands behind his back, looking for something to grab, but he's already going so fast and hard that I have difficulty holding on.

My breath's short, I feel my insides start to spasm, and a heat runs through my entire body. "No, bunny, you come when I tell you to." His hand comes to rest on my mouth to cover my screams. "I knew you were made for me, created and molded to be by my side. " I smile at him, but I'm taken by surprise when he picks me up, like I weigh nothing, and spins me around; I drop with a short breath on my stomach. He grabs my butt cheeks in each of his hands and spreads them apart. "That ass is mine." I feel a finger go along my slit and stop right on my hole. I move and try to escape the intrusion. "No. Cam. No!"

With his strong muscles and that hand on my back, I can't even budge. And I feel the curious finger leave the skin, but before I can breathe a sigh of relief, I hear him suck something, and he puts it right back on my asshole. Wet. "I said no!" He pushes the end of his digit a little more and starts to enter. "I know no means yes, little bunny, as long as you don't use your safe word. That's our game." Fuck he's right. Do I want to use it? Do I want to play? When his finger goes into the first knuckle, I shut the fuck up and tense a little bit, closing my eyes. As I stop thrashing, he pulls his hand off my back and goes straight to cup my pussy. "Oh fuck, Fallon, you're making a mess of my bed." Pressing his palm on my core, he starts massaging vigorously, and I forget the finger in my ass. "I'm going to take my finger out. But remember that ass," He bends down and bites one of my cheeks so hard I stick my face into the mattress to contain my scream. "Is mine. And I'm going to break it. Not now. But soon." Without warning, his imposing cock is back inside me, and I let out a cry of pleasure that doesn't even sound like my own voice. He's holding my hip so hard I can feel the bruises forming on me. His other hands go straight to my chin, and he grips it tightly, shoving his middle finger into my mouth. I greet him with my teeth before letting him push it deeper. He's pumping hard, and I can't control my moans; it's so fucking good. Drools pooling in my mouth, I feel it drip down the corner and on his hands. I closed my lips and sucked hard his finger, swallowing my saliva.

His face is a few inches away from mine; he turns my face so I can see him. I know he can see me through the mask, but I'm confronted with the sight of a monster, a killer. With a few last deep and violent trust, he stops before emptying himself entirely inside me, and I take the wave too, living my orgasm, milking the rest of his.

CHAPTER 22

INVISIBLE CHAINS

FALLON

I can hardly believe what's happening as Camden takes me in his arms and leads me to the shower. He's so gentle with me like he's cradling a delicate flower, and it surprises me. Each time we are together, it starts with fire and passion and ends with care and confusion.

He gently places me on the toilet seat and starts turning on the shower. Everything feels so sudden and unexpected. I'm trying to figure out what the fuck I'm doing. Water starts to flow, and I realize he's probably planning to give me a shower. It's all happening so fast, and I'm just here, taking it all in. He approaches me again, taking my hands in his, and I follow.

The warm, soothing water cascades over us. His gentle touch massages my back and shoulders, kneading away the tension that had been building ever since I first stepped into this cursed manor. His fingers dug deep, finding stress knots and releasing them into the steamy air. It's a moment of bliss, peace, and clarity, and I feel my body finally relaxing after all this time. The combination of the hot water and Camden's care erased all my worries, and I feel like I'm in heaven.

His fingers gently brush my scalp, and my head lolls forward as I let out a sigh of relief. Camden moves to my face, his digits lightly tracing my jawline, and I feel his breath on my forehead. I look up to find his eyes on mine. He doesn't say a word, but I can feel the intensity of his emotions as he looks at me. His loving embrace is slowly breaking down the walls I've built up around my heart. His hands run over me as he washes away the sweat and blood from my body. He explored my body, leaving a trail of goosebumps in his wake, each touch sending a wave of pleasure through me. My eyes drifted shut as his lips ghosted light kisses along my shoulders and neck. I feel safe in his embrace, and his gentle caresses lulled me into a peaceful state of mind. He enveloped me in a toasty towel, his gentle hands wrapping me up in its warmth. Taking great care, he lifted me out of the shower, his touch reassuring. Who is this man? Where's the killer?

He breaks the tranquility of the steamy air-filled bathroom when he opens the door and walks toward the bed. "Are you all right?" his voice was like velvet. I nodded, unable to find the words to express anything that's on my mind. He sits on the bed, looks at me smiling, and takes my hands in his. Still, on his lap, I lock my eyes with his, feeling a deep connection between us. His face is a few inches away from mine, and I perceive weird things happening in my damn heart.

"Mine." His hoarse voice echoes through the room even though the volume he used was a whisper. "I'll have to leave in the night. You have to stay here. Without sticking your fucking nose all over the place. Just....wait for me." He adds. Still holding my face tightly, his blue eyes look into mine, searching for an answer from me. But my mind has far too many questions to simply acquiesce to his command. I hate order anyway. "Why do you have to leave?" He smiles and places a kiss on my forehead before rolling onto his back and looking at the ceiling. "To kill, bunny." My stomach rolls a little, and my heart races.

In our moment of passion, I forgot the details of the horrors he mentioned earlier, but now everything comes crashing back to me. "Who are you going to kill, Cam?" He grunts and squints his eyes as he smiles a little to the side, and he looks fucking gorgeous, lying shirtless in front of me. I put the tip of my index finger on his chest and start tracing the snake tattoo.

"An informant is manifesting to me recently. He put me on the trail of one of the biggest suppliers of children for Franco. And tonight, they have a meeting at our location where the surgeons are. The hospital in Death Valley."

I'm impressed. This one sentence got my eyes filled with water—the idea of seeing children locked in containers, waiting to be butchered into pieces. But Camden said this to me without taking his eyes off the ceiling, without a trace of emotion in his voice. I keep the silence alive for an eternity, continuing my journey along the giant python that wound its way around his body. His eyes met mine as my fingers ran along one of its nipples. "Why is your snake so big?" I asked, curiosity fueling my words. In an instant, his eyes dulled, and his light disappeared. "To hide horrors, Fallon," he murmured solemnly. He got up swiftly to dress himself. "You can stay on this side of the wing. I'll be back as soon as I can." I roll my eyes and sigh heavily at the same time. He leaves the room quickly.

I wonder if he would have stayed longer if I hadn't asked him about his tattoo. I feel bad. When the words left my mouth, he looked like he had seen a ghost. No. I'm not going to dwell over my fate all night and wait for him like a good little animal. That's not my style.

I get up with a determined step and walk quickly to the door that leads to the wing of the house where my room is. Taking care to avoid attention, I quickly enter and rummage through my closet to find clothes that will go unnoticed in the dark. I have to know. I have to see with my own eyes. I have to help.

I follow Camden into the night, my heart racing with mixed emotions. Anger that he thought he could order me around like some puppet, but also a little bit of hurt that he asked me to stay home. I refuse to be weak and let myself be bossed around. My black leggings hug my curves, and my sleek ponytail swishes against my back as I move. I keep my distance, not wanting to be spotted, but close enough to keep an eye on him. I'm determined to see with my two eyeballs what he'll do. I see Camden sneaking down the back alley toward the garage, and I follow him carefully. I have no idea what I'm getting myself into, but I have to. He gets into his car, and I hide behind a bush. With my heart beating way too fast, I watch him settle inside before starting and leaving.

I get up and run quickly into the garage to grab some keys, the first I can find. "What the fuck are you doing?" I stop dead in my tracks and shrug my shoulders. Daniel. "I have to follow Cam. He may need some help." Daniel looks at me with his intimidating posture and powerful masculinity. "Fallon. He clearly doesn't want you to be involved in any of this." I open my arms and move quickly, trapping the behemoth in front of me in a hug. "Danny boy. I need to do something." He grabs me by the shoulders and gently pulls me back. "Did he tell you everything?" I nod. "I have to go, or I'll lose track of him." My voice is a plea, almost like a little girl's wanting a lollipop. "There's no way you're going alone. I'll drive you. I know where he's going." I raise my eyebrows in surprise. But chooses not to push my luck and remains silent.

Driving inside a black truck, I look out the window at the scenery. It's late, and the city seems asleep. But when we finally get close to the destination, Daniel gives me a little tap on the shoulder and points with his chin in front of us. I focus my gaze and see a path that seems to lead nowhere. "Where are we going?" Daniel seems nervous. "Into hell, Fallon." I swallow hard and look at the side of his impassive face.

His hand stretches effortlessly to the glove compartment in front of me. He opens it and pulls out a knife, a magnificent weapon that seems to be made for hunting. He hands it to me. "Take this. Just in case. It's a gift." My trembling hands take the blade, and I struggle to hold back my tears. Despite all the fathers-in-law I've had in my life, none of them have made my heart feel a trace of love. But Daniel, after all these weeks I've been with him, the car trips, the jokes, and now this attention, Daniel makes me feel appreciated. He acts with me like a father, in a way, taking care of me and worrying.

"Love you, Danny boy," I say softly. He looks at me and smiles. "Don't cry, you're going to make me cry." And on that note, he takes a turn in the desert to place the truck behind a rock and shuts down the engine. "Are you ready?" "Always, with you and Cam by my side."

CHAPTER 23

ANY COST

CAMDEN

I press my body low, tucking into the shadow cast by the towering metal containers. Man, this desert cold is seeping right through my clothes, giving me those chills. Tonight feels all kinds of eerie, and my dad's words keep playing in my head. *You are useless, the product of a rape I did with one of the whores I sold to a wealthy man. You are a piece of shit. I hate you.* I shut my eyes tight, knowing tonight's the night everything comes to a head. Under this dark sky, our family's name will take the last hit. Over the years, I created a persona with my skeleton. Killed everyone joining the enterprise. And now, I'm finally at the stage to put an end to it. I adjust the mask on my face, the one I use each time I cleanse the world of another vile member of their heinous circle. I'm the reaper they never see coming, and tonight's harvest will be mine.

I watch from the shadows as Franco, surrounded by his personal bodyguards, mingles with a group of men illuminated under the harsh lights beside the hospital. No sound escapes the scene, but the silent dialogue is deafening: the nods, the handshakes, the predatory sizing up of allies and foes. My fingers twitch in anticipation. I've waited for this, prepared for the moment when I will end the trafficking that courses through the veins of the Betto empire like poison. With every beat of my heart, I vow to tear it all down, to reduce their operation to ashes, no matter the cost.

I creep. The ground beneath my feet feels charged with a silent promise of violence. The air is thick with the smell of blood yet to be spilled. I relish it, a scent that speaks to my soul. My movements are slow and deliberate, the anticipation of the hunt heightening every sense. A guard, separated from the flock, I stopped and watched his face; he seemed to have heard a distant noise. As he peels away to investigate, my lips curl into a smirk. My target is now weakened by one. Crouched low, I pause in the shadow, fucking hesitation grabs me. What was that fucking sound he heard? Resisting the urge to curse aloud, I let a low sigh through my clenched jaw. Fuck. I've been on the hunt for those traffickers with a clear mission in mind. But now, even though I know I should stay on track, I find myself drifting. It's an unexpected turn, but something is pulling me towards it. I turn, a blend of irritation and intrigue turning my steps towards the hospital. Something in the marrow of my bones whispers that it's more than just the wind as the hospital grows bigger as I get closer, its shape dominating the dark sky. I brace myself, unsure of what's ahead. A dark determination takes over, enveloping my purpose like a cloak. Whatever's hiding in that building's corners, I'm geared up to confront it.

Leaning against the old, damp wall, my rifle feels

cold and comfortable in my grip, an extension of the rage boiling within me, pointing in front of me. The corridor stretches out, its decrepit state a reflection of the vile operation it hides. Each step I take is measured, my resolve hardening with the shadows that dance along the crumbling walls. The shadow I've been trailing vanishes into a room up ahead. As the silent cry of an attack pierces the stillness, a bolt of adrenaline shoots through me. My footsteps quicken, the need to act sharpening within me like a honed blade. Rounding the corner, my eyes lock onto the scene, a tableau of blood and retribution. Fallon stands, a figure of wrath and beauty, her hands-stained crimson. On the floor lies the guard, his throat silenced by her. The sight stirs something in me. And, like, each time she's near, I'm fucking hard. I'm frozen in place, taking in the intensity of the moment. Fallon's breathing is uneven, her eyes reflecting the raw intensity of what she's done. There's this palpable tension in the air, mixing the metallic scent with the electricity of our shared mission. The determination we've built hangs thickly between us, a connection solidified by our commitment to this dark cause. I'm fucking mad at her for being here, and for a moment, I'm utterly still, caught in the gravity of it all. Without a word, I step forward. My own voice is a ghost, barely a whisper, "What are you doing here, bunny?" Fallon's eyes ablaze with the sensation I know too much, taking a life, lock onto mine. Silence wraps around us, not peaceful, but charged, like the sky before a storm. I smell her anger, desire, and something fiercer. "I swear I'm going to fucking punish you for coming here," I growl, the words barely a whisper but laden with a finality that resonates in the tight space between us. Fallon doesn't flinch, doesn't speak. Yet her silence screams volumes, echoing my own vow back at me. I grab one of his bloody hands and bring it up to my face; with my other hand, I pull my mask up to my nose, leaving my mouth uncovered. Placing one of Fallon's fingers closer to my face, I examine it before locking eyes with her. "I…I wanted to help you. But... I was supposed to stay hidden. But… He saw me." Her voice is low, calm, and composed. Daniel bursts through the door, his entrance brash, frantic, shattering the stillness. His eyes dart between us, gun in hand. Caught up in the intensity of the moment, Daniel's urgent voice breaks through, "We have to move. Now!"

But his urgency fades, overshadowed by the strong pull of desire and an instinctual urge deep in me. "Leave Daniel. " My voice is authoritative. It's an order. I'm beyond salvation, spiraling down into the depths where only Fallon can follow. And I'll take us both down into the abyss if it means she's with me at any cost.

CHAPTER 24

BULLET RAIN

FALLON

The harsh buzz of fluorescent lights fills the room, casting a pale glow over our faces. Panic twirls wildly in Daniel's eyes, a silent scream for me to intervene. With the slightest quiver of my chin in affirmation, I silently give him the go-ahead to go, to do what has been asked of him by Camden. Without hesitation or argument, Daniel complies, his figure retreating quickly, leaving me standing alone with Camden. The guard lies motionless at our feet, a reminder of the life I just took. His radio, still attached to his belt, sporadically bursts to life with anxious voices, their tones sharp with concern as they seek out the whereabouts of their comrade.

There's this moment, this fucked up, the twisted realization that hits me, I've taken a life. And I feel nothing except this raw, screaming desire for Camden that's clawing at my insides like it's trying to break free. "You want to chase little bunny? OK. But don't die. Otherwise, I'm going to have to slit my own fucking throat and go pick you up in heaven to bring you down with me."

I follow Camden's lead. We dart through the shadows, silent as ghosts, avoiding the spill from the wall light. He's clearly in his element, and I'm his unlikely accomplice, adrenaline surging with each synchronized step we take. The sound of guards shouting in the distance is getting louder and closer.

Camden pushes a heavy pistol into my palm; its weight is foreign and ominous. "Do exactly as I do," he whispers. We slide along the walls; the chaos behind us is swelling, and the guards' hurried footsteps create a quick, urgent beat, pushing us to move faster. We slip into a room with a window overlooking the scene outside. My pulse thrashes in my ears as I catch sight of the targets, Franco and the distributor, oblivious to the strings about to be cut. Camden assembles a sniper rifle with a surgeon's precision, the parts clicking into place, quiet and deadly.

He's a phantom in the dim light, a harbinger of death in his own home. "If the guards come in here, which is almost inevitable, I'll kill them, but you don't have the choice; you shoot," he instructs, voice steady as a heartbeat.

He expects me to be his backup, to hold his life in my hands. The room is silent save for our breathing and the distant shouting. My senses heighten, and the weird taste of fear is clear on my tongue. My fingers curl around the pistol's grip, and I peer through the window. The sight of the gathering below sends a shiver down my spine. This is the reality of my choices, the world I've stepped into. There's no going back now.

Careful not to make a sound, I slide along the wall, my gaze fixed on Camden. His eyes are on the window, vigilant as ever. He doesn't spare me a glance, but I can feel his awareness of my every move, a silent watchman.

The plan's simple but risky: avoid the gunshots in the hospital, stay alive, and in the shadowed corner of the room, my mind races with plans. If I can get close enough to one of those bastards, a knife to the throat might do the trick, silent, deadly, and far more personal.

As I settle into position, right next to the door, the rifle's weight secured in the waistband of my pants, my senses sharpen, the world narrowing down to the space between my heartbeat and the next breath. The anticipation of violence hangs heavy. Camden stays concentrated, the shape of his jaw beneath the mask showing his determination. I can't help but admire the lethal grace in his person. We're a fucked-up duo, playing with lives like it's nothing more than a twisted game.

And yet, despite the situation, an almost perverse thrill courses through my veins, igniting every nerve ending. Danger has a peculiar way of turning fear into something else, something dark and exciting. It's vile, but it's the truth. We're alive in these moments, more so than ever.

I catch my reflection in a sliver of glass on the floor. The sight snaps my focus back—time to get my head in the game. I tighten my grip on the knife. Ready to strike, to end another life. Quick. Clean. Efficient. It's the only way out. A silent prayer escapes me as I brace for impact. What a fucking night. Camden's fingers twitch on the trigger, his body tensed like a coiled spring ready to explode. I can't see what he's aiming at, but the tension in the air is thick enough to slice. Suddenly, a shadow stirs from the other side of under the door. I hear a rustling, a soft murmur of the fabric against the fabric, and my breath stills in my chest.

In my next heartbeat, the door swings open with a creak that pierces the silence like a scream. A guard steps through, oblivious to the predator lying in wait. I don't hesitate. My arm whips out, a viper's strike, my fist connecting with the soft flesh of his throat. The guard's eyes bulge, his gasp cut short as blood spurts from the wound, warm and coppery as it splashes onto my face.

He crumples to the ground with a sickening thud, his body going limp. I grab him by the collar, dragging him inside before anyone else notices. My hands are slick with his blood, a macabre glove that seals my act of violence. I slam the door shut, my heartbeat echoing the finality of the lock clicking into place. I look up to find Camden smiling at me rapidly and turning his head right in front of his snipper; in a fraction of a second, I see him press the trigger. Gunshots echo from outside, tearing through the darkness, searching for a target. Instinctively, I duck and press myself against the chilling wall. The rapid bursts of gunfire resonate deeply within me, creating a frenzied rhythm that fuels my adrenaline.

My breath comes out in short bursts, steam in the chilling night air, not like the heat that's pumping through my veins like liquid fire. Camden's back muscles ripple under his shirt as he rolls away from the window and next to me. I don't need to see his face to know he's pissed, the air around him practically crackling with his fury. "FUCK! " He spins towards me, and I'm caught. His eyes find mine, fierce blue whirlpools that pull me in and won't let go. "Are you ok? " he growls, his hands flying over my body in search of injuries.

I want to tell him to calm down. But his touch, god, his touch is electric, scorching trails over my skin and leaving me aching for more. It's a fierce and possessive thing, Camden's hands on me, as if he could will away any harm with just a touch. But as fast as he rolls next to me, he's moving, all raw power and determined fury. He yanks open the door, his silhouette a dark promise against the dim light spilling out from inside. I'm getting up and following right behind him, my anger a living thing.

As he strides into danger without a single fuck to give, I can smell it, the scent of death and, beneath that, the vile stench of fear. But it's not ours. No, because Cam is moving like death toward the little army in here, and they don't stand a chance.

He fires his gun, the sounds deafening in the confined space. Every bullet is a statement, a declaration in the language of violence that he speaks so fluently. I can't help but follow his lead, my own trigger finger itching to join the symphony of destruction. The rush is real. The need to survive is primitive and raw, a call of the wild that resonates down to my core. With Camden at my side, I'm invincible.

This isn't just a fight. It's a ballet of bullets and blood orchestrated by the most dangerous maestro I've ever known. The corridors reek of piss and vomit, a result of men crying and begging the man in front of them to spare their lives. But it's useless; he walks, arms outstretched, and shoots. Kill everyone who gets in our way. Bodies lie scattered, the aftermath of a brutal purge, their lifeless eyes staring into nothingness.

Camden turns to me, breathless from the carnage. Exhaustion clings to his frame as he rips off his mask, a gesture of finality, and tosses it to the bloodstained floor. It lands with a soft thud. I close the gap between us, driven by a force as primal as the violence we've dispensed.

Jumping into his arms, our bodies collide, a clash of adrenaline and raw emotion. His lips crash against mine, a passionate kiss that tastes of vengeance and the dark oath. He pins me against the wall, our ragged breaths mingling as he grinds against me, a hard arousal pressing insistently.

CHAPTER 25

NEED A HAND

FALLON

Camden's hands work over my body, fierce and demanding, like he's trying to claim every part of me. It's all teeth and tongue, raw hunger, with each bruising kiss and rough caress in the dim corridor of the hospital. But there's a burn beneath my skin, a kind of need that's almost agonizing in its intensity. Camden pulls back quickly, a slight crease marring his brow.

He looks down the hall, eyes narrow, alert. There's something about the way he holds himself like an apex predator sensing danger. I notice it, too, a guard on the floor, not quite as lifeless as we thought. Camden's motion is swift as he lowers me to the ground. His movements are calculated, the embodiment of controlled violence as he approaches the slowly dying man. "Look, bunny. We have one alive."

"Fu…fuck y…you. " The man spits in Cam's direction. My breath catches in my throat, the scent of antiseptics in the air now mixed with the faint coppery smell of blood. "I don't like the idea of someone trying to hurt my wife, you see," Cam says, leaning over the guard. Hearing him call me his wife takes me by surprise, but fuck, I like it.

"I really fucking hate it. Makes me want to burn the goddamn world." Camden kneels beside him, a blade glinting in his hand. His eyes meet mine, a silent question, a dare. Time seems to slow, the moment stretching out as he presses the edge against the man's wrist. I'm frozen, anticipation and dread mingling in a sickening cocktail as the guard lets out an agonized scream. My body responds, a twisted surge of arousal at the macabre scene unfolding before me. Each glance he hurled in my direction carried an unbearable weight: need, admiration, love. Can he love?

The knife in his hands was an extension of his steely will, its sharp edge gleaming with malice under the harsh lights. With each precise incision, the steel carved into flesh, bones, and all. The man's screams echoing off the walls. I'm breathing hard; this tense sexual moment between life and death, pain and pleasure, binds Camden and me. It's dark, it's dirty, and in some fucked up way, it feels right.

My lips parted, but no sound came out. The guard's cries fade to whimpers, and my heart pounds in time with his labored breathing. I'm a part of this now, complicit in this brutal ballet.

Camden's command is a sinister whisper that wraps around me, "Take off your pants, bunny." The coldness in his voice cuts through the dimly lit room, a razor's edge poised at my psyche, the metallic taste of fear tangling with a conflicting surge of rebellion. The fabric slides over my legs, and I throw them aside.

"Get on your knees for me now." I shiver, not from the cold, but from the realization of my own fucking compliance. My body responds before my mind forms any protest, sinking down until the chill of the floor seeps into my bones.

His imposing figure stands like a quiet storm, and I find myself in the calm center amidst the pauses between his commands. "Now the top," he instructs, and I feel the air catch in my throat. A spiral of heat unfurls within me as I peel away my shirt. Naked, I kneel beside the now unconscious man. Blood pools around him. The scent, rich and metallic, clings to my nostrils while the stickiness brushes against my skin.

Camden's looking right at me. His stare's intense, pulling me in and freaking me out at the same time. The silence is broken by Camden's next command, "Stay." It's an anchor, a rope that binds me to the blood-soaked floor. And I fucking obey because, at this moment, I am the instrument, and he, the maestro of a symphony too dark to name. The room feels smaller, the walls closing in as if they, too, are complicit in this twisted rite. I am Fallon, yet I am becoming something else, a creature forged in the furnace of Camden's will. "So strong, my little bunny."

He doesn't touch me, yet I feel him everywhere, an oppressive force that caresses without contact. I close my eyes, a psychological seduction that leaves me frayed and breathless. "Such a good girl for me." I stand frozen, every muscle tensed, waiting for what comes next. Camden's frame casts a shadow over me.

He leans down, picking up the guard's severed hand. The blood on his fingers tells a dark tale, yet the gentle way he handles the hand contrasts sharply with the brutality of his deed. He brings the cold, ghostly fingers toward me, sliding them between my thighs with a roughness that makes my heart stutter in fear and forbidden anticipation. "Going to show you," he growls, his voice a dark melody of promised retribution. "Going to teach you what happens when someone tries to claim what's mine." He speaks in the direction of the guard, consciousness clawing him back to reality. " In this case, your life." The man stirs, and I hear the soft sobs that escape his lips, a pathetic testament to his helplessness. But it's Camden's smile that chills me most, a twisted display of delight at the suffering he's doing. He guides the guard's hand, the fingers tracing a path along my most intimate parts, a perverse puppeteer. I feel the cold touch of the disembodied limb like a specter's caress, a reminder of the life swiftly departing from the guard, leaving an icy trail of dread along my skin. The guard's weeping grows quieter, but the sound burrows into me, echoing the turmoil that churns within the depths of my being. It's a symphony of horror, playing just for me, the melody pulsing in time with the cold fingers that invade the space where only Camden is allowed. "You tried to kill her sooner." His severe voice directly addresses the man on the ground.

A suppressed scream fights to break from my throat, but I stifle it, my mind teetering on the edge of sanity. My flesh recoils from the dead touch, even as a perverse heat blooms in me. The sensation is macabre, an unholy communion of life and death. Camden's voice is a whisper of silk across sandpaper, "That's it, baby. Feel it." His words seep into my pores, coating me with an invisible film of filth that no scrubbing could remove. I'm tainted, marked by his depravity in this godforsaken temple of healing. My soul may weep for salvation, but it's my body that responds to the blasphemy, branded forever by the cold hand of punishment and Camden's dark, insatiable hunger.

Camden moves with purpose, his hand slamming forcefully against the man's chest. He leans in close, whispers meant for my ears only. "Come closer, Fallon." His order, a velvet threat, sends a shiver down my spine.

I approach on all fours. "Sit on his chest." His voice is sharp. I hesitate for a moment, but the dark promise in his eyes compels me. I do as I'm told, feeling the painful rise and fall of the man's breath beneath me, feeling powerful and powerless all at once.

Camden's smile is a slash in the darkness, filled with malice. He turns to face the man, "What's it like, seeing death so close? She's beautiful, isn't she?" His smile grew wider. "Knowing you touched her but couldn't feel it?" The man's eyes are wide, filled with terror. I almost taste his fear, metallic and tangy on my tongue. Impossible to restrain myself, I close my eyes and roll my hips on the man's chest, feeling my need growing between my legs.

Camden placed a knife in my hand, and I came back to reality. The handle is cool, the weight of it substantial and frighteningly real. "Do it," he commands. My hand quivers wildly, the tremors beyond my control as I clutch the knife's handle with a death-like grip. I inch the razor-edged blade closer to the man's exposed throat, pausing ever so briefly as the icy steel kisses his soft flesh. My heartbeat thunders, deafening me. I brace my resolve and then, with a resolute thrust, slice deeply through the flesh of his throat. Blood surges in a macabre geyser, its grisly warmth dousing my skin, painting me in a sanguine hue. The room whirls, tainted by the scent of metal, the air heavy with the pungent tang of iron that relentlessly assaults my senses.

A bead of the man's essence manages to breach my lips, the coppery flavor lingering with a morbid allure. Covered in the disturbing marks of my actions, I feel connected to the deep darkness that has consumed Camden's spirit entirely. A truth emerges in my mind: we're both creatures of the night, bound by its power.

The man I just silenced lies still beneath me, his life seeping away onto the cold, sterile floor of the hospital. My naked skin feels every splatter and every drip of his blood, a visceral baptism of my own making. I raise my gaze, my eyes entwined with the blue ones in front of me. He is brimming with a pride that ignites a spark deep within me. The world fades in the stillness of our connection, leaving only the thrumming pulse of my yearning heart.

A whisper escapes my lips, a silent plea for him to fucking take me right here and there, my breath carrying the weight of unbridled need. Camden, a statue before me, holds my stare. So, fucking beautiful. His words fall like a gauntlet, "Beg for it, bunny," each syllable a key turning locks in me I had not known existed.

The room seems to shrink with the sheer intensity of his presence, an aura of dominance emanating from him like a deity encased in flesh and blood. My soul unfurls in silent pleas, wordlessly invoking the tempest of his possession. With a commanding grasp, he captures my chin, and in an act that treads the fine line between shame and closeness, he spits in my open mouth. A fire burns intensely inside me, fueled by a deep desire that can't wait to be satisfied and the rage of the humiliation. Then comes the unexpected sting of his palm against my cheek, an acute punctuation to the tender utterance that slips from his lips. "You are breathtaking," he murmurs, and with those simple words, my restraint crumbles into dust.

Overwhelmed by the moment's intensity, I surge up from my position, driven by a force that feels beyond my control. With a fierce shove, I send Camden reeling back, his balance undone by the unexpected assault. He topples, his muscular frame tripping over the inert bodies beneath us, and he falls to the cold ground with a heavy thud on his back. I don't waste a second. I pounce on him, straddling his hips with a ferocity that matches the frenetic pounding of my heart. My hands are frantic, fumbling as I struggle to remove his pants, my fingers shaking with a wild urgency that betrays my desperate need for him. This moment is mine, a culmination of raw emotion and untamed impulses. I surrender to the chaos, allowing it to wash over me like a relentless tide, powerful and inexorable. And in the eye of this storm, I discover a truth that leaves no room for doubt: I am undeniably, unashamedly, inexorably intertwined with Camden. Every fiber of my being screams this absolute certainty, and with him, I am more alive than I have ever been.

CHAPTER 26

DIRTY FLOOR

CAMDEN

Fallon, my fierce-as-hell step-sis, looking like a wild thing unleashed. Naked and bloody, she's pure, unadulterated sin, and she's got my dick harder than a coffin nail. She pounces, a panther in human skin, her grip on my gear fierce and hungry. With a yank that rips the fabric, my shirt, jeans, and boxers are history. My cock springs free, proud, and more than ready for whatever hell we're about to raise. This woman has an appetite that's off the charts, and my body's starving for her.

Every inch of me is screaming to flip the script, to take control and show her how the game's played. But there's something about the way she's clawing for me, desperate and fierce, that's got me letting her call the shots for now. This is fucking love. I don't want to think it's anything else.

There she is, hovering over me like some dark angel in a fucked-up painting. Her face is close, too damn close, and I feel the heat rolling off her pussy right onto my hard-on. It's sinful, the way my blood's pumping, responding to her without permission. I let out a low growl at the sensation, my hips betraying me with the tiniest of fucking movements, sending her eyes rolling back. Shit. "Kiss me," she breathes, her lips practically begging for it.

I've never been about that tender shit. I grab her face in my hands, thumb tracing her cheek, and lay it out for her plain and simple, "Never been gentle, never took the time for kisses." But my fucked-up bunny, she's insistent, like she's trying to carve out a new slice of Camden just for herself. "Maybe it's time. For me," she says, with that fire in her eyes that's fucking with my head. "Fallon," I tell her, my voice all gravel and smoke, "I'd do anything for you."

And before I can rethink the shit coming out of my mouth, we're locked in this passionate, raw, first-time kiss that's got fire licking through my veins. Nothing about this feels like me, and yet it feels exactly like what I've been missing. It's wild, it's crazy, and it's the kind of passion that could either burn us to the ground or light up the whole goddamn sky. Her kiss, a molten clash of tongues and teeth, tastes like survival and fucking madness.

I flipped her, and she fell on her back directly on the floor. "Again." She looks at me, confused. "Kiss me again, bunny." Her face finds mine immediately, her lips soft and reassuring. I wedge myself between her thighs, teasing her wet pussy with my fingertips. "Fuck, Fallon, you're dripping for me," I growl, sliding a finger deep inside her. She clenches around it, and it's all the answer I need.

I commit myself to ensure her satisfaction, skillfully leading her toward her climax and steadily amplifying her longing. At the right moment, I stop. My laughter reverberates through the room, a symphony of sin and satisfaction. She's pissed, and I bring my finger coated with her slick, warm juice to my mouth. Lick them clean and trace her skin.

I feel that shiver running through her. It's a power trip. She's like some wild thing, and I got to admit, it gets me. I'm on my knees, towering above her perfect body.

"Camden, what the hell are you doing?" Fallon breathes out, her voice thick with need and anger. Laughing, I lean in closer, my mouth just inches from her ear. "I'm getting my favorite meal," I whisper, letting my breath tickle her. And I watch as goosebumps spread over her skin like wildfire. Am I pushing her too far by denying her orgasm? Maybe, but that's half the fun.

My hands are greedy now, sliding over every inch of her. "Camden, stop fucking teasing me," Fallon growls, and I have to chuckle because she's so damn honest and raw. So, I do the only thing that feels right. I take my cock in hand and guide it inside her, her wetness making it all too easy.

Still with my back straight, I rub my dick along her slit, closing her eyes to the sensation of friction. Breathing harder, I only push the tip inside, and my head falls back. I repeat the movement, deliciously slowly, several times.

The mix of pleasure and something close to pain etched across her face is almost too much to handle. It's like she's fighting herself just as much as she's fighting me, and I don't know if I want to stop it or push it even further. "Fuck, Camden, just do it already," she hisses, and that's all the invitation I need.

With a deliberate and powerful thrust, I bury myself deep in her, claiming her entirely. Her eyes clamp shut, her lip caught between her teeth in an attempt to suppress the sounds of her pleasure. But I have other intentions. "Look at you. Taking me so well," I murmur to her, my voice a blend of commendation and carnal promises. "Good girl. "

We become an entangled chaos of limbs and burning desire on the floor as the first light of day begins to seep into the room. The experience is primal and unyielding. At this moment, she belongs to me. I belong to her. Consumed by the intensity of our shared passion. Each motion, every powerful thrust, becomes a poignant declaration of the fierce bond we share. Our bodies are in perfect harmony, a dance of passion that ignites with each touch, each gasp for air.

Every push, every pull is a silent vow of this unspoken bond, our heartbeats drumming in rhythm. My back arches, straight as an arrow; I look down at her, fucking perfect. Sprawled beneath me on those delicate fucking elbows. My hands greedy, demanding, they reach for her pulsing heat. I place it on her pussy, spreading my fingers wide, leaving enough space for my cock to glide between. Feeling her, hearing her, smelling her, I'm losing my fucking mind.

The smacking sound of flesh on flesh, that wet, slapping noise that tells me she's as lost in this as I am. I'm hyper-aware of her under me, the flex of her back, the sweat gleaming on her skin. She's a sight to behold, a vision of sin that's got my blood singing in my veins. I feel my cock, pushing into her, sinking deep into that tight, slick pussy. It's fucking intoxicating the way she clenches around me. "Fuck. Feeling my cock entering you is driving me mad."

She's on fire, and I can't get enough of the heat. My fingers work her pussy, spreading wider, my thumb circling her clit as I thrust into her with a force that has both of us spiraling. It's a relentless rhythm, a claiming that has my name etched into every moan that spills from her lips.

And fuck, the way she looks, those eyes that tell me she knows what she's doing to me. It's a battle, a power play where we're both determined to come out on top. I'm driven, lost in the tactile bliss of our bodies joining. "Mine." I can't stop watching, can't tear my eyes away from the connection of our bodies, the sight of my cock disappearing inside her again and again. It's the rawest thing I've ever seen.

The sound of our bodies slapping together, the feel of her wetness coating me, it's a sensory overload that has my head spinning. Our moans fill the room, a symphony that echoes off the walls. Fallon bites her lip, her eyes flashing with that defiant spark that drew me to her in the first place. She challenges me without saying a word, and it's a fucking turn-on like no other. Gritting my teeth, I push her limits, driving deeper, harder, watching the way her body stretches to accommodate me. She's on the brink. I can feel it. The way her muscles flutter around me that's the signal I've been chasing.

I shift, angling my thrusts to hit just the right spot, determined to push her over the edge. "My goddess." We're a tangle of limbs, a dirty duo locked in blood and filth. The smacking sound grows louder, more desperate, as we both chase the release that's been building since the moment we started this game. It's close. We're teetering on the precipice, hearts racing, sweat mingling as we spiral out of control.

With a final, guttural moan, I push us both over the edge into the abyss of pleasure where nothing matters but the blissful sensation of coming together, hard and unforgiving, on the floor of this hell of a place. And as we shatter into a million fucking pieces. After our moment of madness, we took the time to get dressed, and I took Fallon on a tour of the hospital. I showed her the corners, the secrets, the corpses. Her beautiful honey-colored eyes filled with sadness. And fuck, it made me even more determined to end Franco's days. You can't hurt my bunny, or I'll chase you to your fucking death. The journey to the mansion was silent. I gave her time to process the shit-ton of information I just shared with her. I'm pissed. The plan almost worked. I managed to shoot a bullet into the distributor's head, but my father managed to escape. Now, he's going to be even more protected. For months, I've been tracking down and killing his collaborators. He already knows that a shadow is after him. But now that he's come so close to death, he'll be extremely cautious. I feel her watching me as I sit inside the car. When I take her hand in mine and look into her eyes, she says, "I want to help. I can help. "

CHAPTER 27

PLANING

FALLON

My thoughts are on fire, racing through me with an intense speed I can't escape. Memories from earlier today keep flashing in my mind, undeniable truths I can't shake off. It feels like I've unleashed something powerful, and there's no turning back. The weight of Camden's disclosures looms over us, reminding us of the grim truth we're dealing with.

As Camden steers us through the night, I sense his intense concentration, focused like a laser on what lies ahead in the dark. With his voice low and unforgiving, he continues to paint a hideous picture of the atrocities committed by the distributors and his father, not just somewhere far and detached, but here, in this city, under our very noses. Robbing innocence, shipping it like cargo, only to end up in places like that hospital.

The hospital... I shiver at the memory. The place where they carve out what they can and discard the rest, all in the name of profit. My stomach turns with a nauseating roll, anger and sorrow churning within me. How can the world be so cruel? How can people like Franco sleep at night?

I can't shake the feeling of being complicit by living under the same roof as the monsters who operate this nightmare. I've seen the containers and heard the stories, but nothing prepared me for the gritty truth Camden laid bare. Kids and women, stolen, used, broken. I feel a surge of rage, a fiery knot in my chest that screams for retribution. I glance at Camden. He's as still as stone.

I'm wondering what it's like to wear it like a second skin. All his life, he lived in it and saw it. Fuck, my heart aches for him, for the kid he used to be. It goes beyond the intrigue of danger now, beyond the forbidden thrill. It's about justice and revenge.

We're going to expose Franco and his depraved empire. We're going to tear it down, brick by brick. And when we do, when the dust settles, and the chains break, maybe we'll find peace. Or perhaps we'll be forever changed, bound by the darkness we've fought so hard to vanquish. I squeeze my hands into fists, nails biting into my palms. I won't let this evil continue, not while I have breath in my body, not while I can stand and fight next to Cam. I turn my gaze to the window, watching the blur of the city pass us by. "I'm with you, Camden," I whisper the words a vow. "Let's burn his empire to the ground." His eyes meet mine briefly, and in them, I see the reflection of my own resolve. We're partners in this now, a duo against the devil. We'll either come out victorious or go down in flames together.

My pulse quickens with a mix of anticipation and

unease as Camden and I work together to gather the last pieces of evidence needed to expose Franco. Every keystroke, every document I review sends a mix of excitement and anxiety coursing through me. We're on the brink, and I can almost feel the triumph, that intense and satisfying sensation of justice. My vision is blurry and tired, the price to pay for looking at computer screens for several days.

The air in Camden's portion of the mansion is thick with silence, punctured only by our steady, purposeful actions. I sense Camden's presence right behind me, a steadfast force filled with determination and ominous purpose, each of his breaths hinting at the danger we both embrace.

The hardest part was leaving him alone during meals and having to eat with Franco and Valentina, all while trying not to raise suspicions. But every time I return to this wing, which now brings me comfort and familiarity, he greets me with passionate kisses, and we dive back into work, trying to devise a new plan.

I glance at Camden, and for a fleeting second, our eyes meet. There's a depth there, a fierce solidarity that speaks louder than any of our fiery clashes. He needs me. And, if I dare admit, I need him too. I suppress the shudder threatening to escape as his hand brushes against mine. His touch is unintentional yet searing.

The screen before us displays the damning evidence, pieces of a puzzle that, once complete, will leave Franco's empire in ruins. But the rush of excitement is quickly drowned by the spike of fear, a fear of what Franco is capable of when cornered. Cam breaks the silence, his voice a low growl that resonates with urgency. "Fallon, this is beyond dangerous now. Understand that once we do this... " He doesn't finish his sentence, but the weight of his unfinished warning wraps around my throat.

My fingers hesitate above the keyboard. This is the point of no return. My heart hammers against my ribcage as if pleading for a reprieve from the impending storm. I look at Camden again, searching his face for some semblance of doubt, but find none. Only the steely man who's been waiting a lifetime to dismantle the tyranny of his own blood. The breath I've been holding escapes in a shaky sigh. "I know," I whisper.

He steps closer, his hand firmly covering mine, our fingers interlaced. His piercing blue eyes lock onto mine. "We do this together, little bunny. No looking back." I nod, the gesture honest but straightforward.

Together, we stand, side by side, outside the windows; the dark sky seems to press against the glass. "Trust no one," he had said weeks earlier, and as the gravity of our actions sinks in, I realize the depth of his warning.

For a moment, we're just two figures hovering in front of the ghostly glow of the computer screen, the shadows of the room stretching out, enveloping us in an embrace that's both protective and suffocating. I can't shake the feeling. It's a visceral tug in my veins, an unspoken plea to linger. Camden's dark, brooding eyes hang onto mine, a storm swirling in those depths. He's made clear he doesn't want me to leave, his stance firm, rooted to the spot as he could somehow will me to stay.

But there's work to be done, dangerous work, and tonight, I have to play the spy once more. "One wrong move and everything could go up in flames," he warns. "I need to do this, Camden," I say, and the weight of truth in those words tugs a knot tighter in my chest.

His hand hovers, a breath away from mine, the air charged with unspoken sentiments. "Be careful, Fallon. You're not alone in this," he adds, and it's those words, that promise, that chase away the chill wrapping around my heart. The plan is clear: the façade of normalcy, my role as the obedient daughter at the family dinner with my mother and that monster Franco. I need to gauge the man's vibe.

I nod, the gesture a seal over our silent pact, and leave Camden behind without a kiss goodbye or even a glance. I find it too difficult. The door closes with a soft click, marking the threshold between the sanctuary we've built and the treacherous path that lies ahead. In Camden's world, even a closed door is an open invitation for danger. With each step towards my side of the manor, I feel my heartbeat sync with the undercurrent of risk that this evening holds. The plan is easy; in theory, endure and observe. But simple things sometimes are really the hardest ones to go through.

The soft bulbs frame my face, casting a pretty glow on my features. I prepare for dinner, catching my reflection in the vanity mirror; I prepare my hair, makeup, and mask of a naive and foolish young woman. The years have trained me well for this. Yet, it's the memory of Cam's intense gaze that centers me, grounding my thoughts in the whirl of adrenaline—the way he makes me feel alive, strong, and powerful.

Franco's eyes are on me at the dinner table, calculating, weird. Next to him, Valentina is as clueless as ever, her quiet laughter a soft chime oblivious to the undercurrents swirling beneath our conversation. I know she's too wrapped up in her own gilded world to notice the clouds that have been gathering ever since we arrived at this opulent prison. But it's the knowledge that Cam is watching over me, his promise echoing, that forges the courage I need to stay sitting, facing the monster. With each clink of silverware, each sip of wine, I thread my way through the façade, my senses heightened to the undercurrents of every exchanged glance, every rehearsed pleasantry. "It seems we don't see you as often, Fallon. What do you do with your days?" Franco asks. "I enjoy going shopping and reading some books," I reply, raising my voice as high as possible, bubbly and cheerful, and Valentina claps her hands. "Aw, that's my girl." But clearly, Franco isn't biting the bait.

His gaze turned stern, and I sensed suspicion in his eyes. Without warning, Daniel's big voice surfaces. "Miss Fallon keeps me in shape. We have to walk constantly. It's good for my cardio." Why is he lying? What does he have to gain by weaving a protective veil over my lies? His eyes catch mine, a brief flicker of something unidentifiable passing through them before he turns back to Franco. A long-term employee playing his role with finesse seems to convince Franco somehow to trust my words. A silent sigh of relief slips past my lips, my shoulders easing down from their tense perch near my ears. It's working.

Franco's edges soften, the suspicion in his gaze dulling into what I can only hope is acceptance. Daniel's intervention has thrown me a lifeline, and I grasp it with both hands, desperate to maintain the façade just a little while longer.

The dinner continues, a subtle ballet of chats and courteous questions, and I go along with it, my heart pounding erratically against my chest. With each word, each smile that doesn't quite reach my eyes, I'm acutely aware of the web of lies I'm tangled in. But there's no turning back now. I'm in too deep, caught in the middle of a deadly game that I can't afford to lose.

"Can I count on you to be present at the ball tomorrow night, Fallon? It would be great to take some photos for social media." Franco asked me. I nod silently. This is perfect. I'll be able to see and take photos of a horrible person. People who buy the organs of innocent children. "It will be a masquerade ball. Your mother bought several masks for you. You'll choose with her. Daniel knows the location and hour. He'll take you." And with his last words, he gets up and leaves the table.

CHAPTER 28

UNKNOWN NUMBER

FALLON

I walked the cold corridors filled with spirits, reflecting on my first days here. Trying to find Daniel, to get some answers, was a flop. The guy's a ghost.

I turn in circles in this room that's supposed to be mine, but it doesn't feel like anything's mine in this place except Cam. This house has everything someone could want if you don't look too into it. But I don't want any of it, and I already know too much. I just want Camden. I want that fire we have, that dangerous spark that threatens to set everything ablaze. I want to be free with him, chase bad guys, and rid the world of them.

I let my body fall into the bed, the mattress swallowing me whole. I'm here, in this room, but I wish I were anywhere else. Fuck, I even start to miss my beat-up apartment in Vancouver. The silence is eating at me when suddenly, my phone buzzes to life. My heart goes off like a gunshot in my chest as I snatch it up. A message. An unknown number. Every part of me says it could be a trap, but what if it's not? What if it's... him?

I hold my breath, my thumb hovering over the screen, and tap the message open. It's Camden. My pulse races and a wild feeling surges through me like a current.

Bunny. You stay in your room.

So authoritative.

So, responding when I am.

I'm on the edge, teetering between what I should do and what I want to do. The mansion may be full of dark corners and unspoken threats, but it's Camden's text message on my screen that's got me feeling like I might just dive into the deep end.

I'm serious. I saw the way Franco looked at you. He knows some thing. Tonight, I'm going out. I'll dig for information.

I want to come.

No bunny. Stay in your nest.

For now.

Will you come to see me after?

Already craving my dick, naughty girl?

Maybe.

No. Not tonight. But be sure I'm watching everything you do.

Stalker

Deranged

Fuck you

You already did, little bunny.

I smile at that. It's dark in my room, the kind of silence you can feel pressing against your skin. My heart's racing, a trapped rabbit against ribcage bars. The message on my phone was stark against the dim glow of the nightstand lamp. *I'm watching everything you do.* The words sear into my thoughts.

I drop the phone, the thud muffled by the carpet, and lay back on the bed, eyes searching the ceiling above as if it holds answers. There are no cameras here; what's he playing at? Pushing away the spiral of thoughts, I roll off the bed, making a quick decision to drown out this unease with water and steam.

Water embraces me in its comforting warmth, cascading over my skin in gentle torrents that follow a soothing rhythm. Steam gently ascends, wrapping around me like a comforting veil made of mist. The droplets move across me, resembling gentle touches from a kind presence, gliding intimately over my skin. With every drop that falls, a weight seems to lift, as if the very essence of my apprehension is being washed away, leaving trails of transient purity that glitter and shimmer before joining the others in their inevitable descent.

The steam still clings to me as I step out of the shower, skin flushed from the heat, heart still pounding with… Annoyance? Arousal? Questions? That bastard. Leaving me behind to go seek information. Telling me he's watching. I shake my head, trying to rid myself of the image of his intensity, his dangerous eyes fixated on me. I'm making scenarios up in my head, and it's fucking annoying.

I stroll across the room, drops of water trailing behind me, goosebumps rising with the cool touch of air. With a nonchalance I'm far from feeling, I slide open the drawer of my bedside table.

And I come face to face, or should I say head, with my dildo. The one I fucked Camden with. Shit, just the thought sets my body aflame with a kind of hunger that could get me done in seconds. I grasp it and walk toward the bed, my fingers tingling with the memory of our twisted, forbidden act. My hand finds its way between my legs, rubbing the length of the fake cock against my folds, each motion igniting more of that fire in me. There's a tempting, wicked edge to this arousal as I picture the way I penetrated Cam's ass with it.

As pleasure intensifies, I can't help it and reach for my knife. The blade is cold and full of promises. It offers a strange kind of solace, a reminder that I can carve my own path, slice through any bullshit that stands in my way. Lying back on the bed, I let my eyes flutter shut, lost in the sensation of the dildo's friction while the knife's blade traces patterns across my neck.

The point dances on my skin, a firm teasing touch and a shiver ripple through me. The blade descends to my inner thigh, the hand between my legs moving in rhythm to the knife's wandering path. The edge presses enough to feel but not enough to cut. Until I push harder, just a bit, it's a risk, but it makes me closer to my climax.

A tiny bead of blood pearls up, and it's the wildest fucking sensation, the pain mixing with pleasure and shattering into ecstasy. I come hard, my body convulsing with the force of it, the blade drawing one last cut from my skin. Fuck. It's sick, it's wrong, and it's about the most honest thing I've felt in this messed-up world of mine. I'm breathless with the thrill of it, my heartbeat a wild drum in my chest.

The world spins, and for a moment, it's like everything fades except the glowing numbers of the bedside clock. Late, way too damn late. I'm exhausted, my body still humming from the buzz. But hell, what a day.

The fabric of my pajama shorts clings to my skin as I settle under the covers. Just as sleep begins to creep in, teasing my weary mind, my phone buzzes a jolt that breaks the silence like a sledgehammer on glass. I reach for it, the light from the screen a harsh intruder in the darkness of my room. With a swipe, I unlock it, and there's a message from the man who makes my life so fucking weird.

Don't ever fuck that dildo again.

The only thing I do is smile. So, he really dared put a camera in my room. The fucker watched me rub myself like a frantic sex depraved women. It's good to know. The mansion is quiet around me as if holding its breath. But I know better. In the quiet, in the dark, that's where the secrets thrive. That's where the snakes like Franco and the enigmatic Camden slither. And I'm caught between them, the unsuspecting prey that grew fangs. A bitter chuckle escapes my lips, the sound sharp and sudden. Maybe, just maybe, I'm the most dangerous of them all. I wake up to the sound of commotion, the feeling like a herd of bulls is busting through my room. I roll over and squint against the bright light flooding in as Mom rips open the curtains. Ugh, before my brain even kicks into full gear, I reach for my phone. No other messages from Camden. My heart sinks a little, but I brush it off.

I'm not about to get all twisted up over some guy, even if that guy is as complicated and electric as him. Mom's got this whole day planned out, appointments stacked on top of each other. All in preparation for the big, fancy masked ball tonight.

You've got to love the irony, a mask to hide the fact that I've been wearing one ever since I stepped foot into this life. Valentina waltzes in, each mask she shows off more elaborate than the last. She's in her element, all but bursting with excitement for the event. Me? I just want to crawl back under the covers and forget about the whole thing. But Mom's having none of it. She's on a mission to get me glammed up and ready to dazzle at the ball.

She tugs at my blankets, and I groan, not ready to face the day. The hustle and bustle of hair stylists, makeup artists, and the designer's critical eye waiting to size me up. The thought alone is exhausting. "Come on, baby! " Still, the commitment's been made, and with the sun glaring down on me, there's no chance to bail. So, with a reluctant sigh, I swing my legs over the edge of the bed, bracing for the flurry of preparations ahead. It's go time, and whether I like it or not, I've got a role to play. Tonight's the night, and every second leading up to it will be spent primping and preening. Ready to put on a show. "We'll have a beautiful day, Fallon baby. " Her enthusiasm seems so genuine; it stole me a little smile.

The gentle purr of Daniel's truck rolls beneath us as we make our way from the hair salon to the makeup artist's place. The bitch hairdresser had the audacity to suggest chopping off my hair. As if I'd let her shear my wavy locks. I'd told her to refresh my blond a little bit and curl it. Sitting beside me, Mom's all dolled up, her own hair done up fancy. But she's as quiet as a church mouse, and it's driving me crazy. I can't stand the silence, the unanswered questions swelling up in my mind like a storm cloud ready to burst. As Daniel navigates the streets, I finally gather the guts to speak up. "Mom," I say, my voice a little shaky, "what's the deal with Franco? I mean, you never talk about him." She tenses, her lips pressed into a thin line that scream, 'Mind your business,' but I'm past caring about boundaries. Franco's this looming figure in our lives, and I'm sick of tiptoeing around the elephant in the room. There's a weight to the air, thick with the tension of my question. It hangs between us, dangling, waiting for an answer that seems never come.

I can see the conflict play across her face, a war of whether to open up or keep me in the dark. The truck slows to a stop outside the makeup artist's studio, but before we can get out, Mom turns to me, her eyes heavy with a story yet to be told. "Fallon," she starts, and I lean in, a cliffhanger hanging in the air, ready to swallow me whole. She opens her mouth, and I brace myself for the truth, ready for the floodgates to open. But she pauses, a hesitation that chokes the confession in her throat, and instead offers a feeble, "We'll talk later, okay?" I'm left hanging, my heart pounding, yearning for an answer that refuses to come. It's frustrating and aggravating, and it makes me want to scream. The truck door opens, and reality comes crashing back. We're ushered out, and the world of glitz and glam wraps around us once more. As I step into the studio, I can't shake the feeling that I'm walking right into the center of a web that's been spun long before I arrived. And why does it feel like the answer lies just beyond my reach?

CHAPTER 29

A DANCE WITH THE DANGER

CAMDEN

I'm parked outside this fucking fancy suit store, staring at my reflection in the rearview mirror. I got to pick up an ensemble and a mask for tonight's shit show because I can't obviously wear the skeleton one. Sitting here, I can't help but replay that scene from last night, Fallon, my goddamn rabid bunny, getting off with that dildo, then slicing her pretty porcelain skin with the blade.

Fuck. Just thinking about it makes me hard again. I was in the middle of squeezing info out of one of Franco's best guys, planning to keep him breathing till he spilled. But my phone buzzes with the special setup for the camera movement detection in Fallon's room, and there she was on the screen, fucking perfect, moaning on her own. The bastard chained to the chair manages to catch a glimpse, and that was a line crossed. No one gets that privilege but me. I had to kill him. My plan's going to hell... again.

I remember gripping that shithead, my hands slick with the sweat of rage, and the fucker wouldn't squeal. His eyes, wide and wild, glanced over at the little bag I'd thrown on the table. I could tell he knew what was coming next. I grabbed the bag, pulling out my tools, a cutter, scissors, and an assortment of blades that glinted under the harsh light. "I'm only going to ask you once, " I warned him, my voice low and cold as the steel in my hand. "Who is going to be the next distributor? "

He tried to be tough, clenched jaw, spitting defiance, but I knew the game better. I'd played it since I was a kid, and I knew all the damn rules. "Fuck you, " he spat, and my fuse lit.

I started small, shallow cuts and a little blood to show him I wasn't messing around. But the bastard held his tongue, so I increased the stakes. The scissors worked their magic, snipping off a finger. His screams filled the room, a symphony to my ears, but still, no words I needed to hear. With each refusal, I took something from him. A cut here, a slice there, until the floor glistened with crimson, and his resolve began to crack. His body was a canvas, and I painted it with the color of agony, a masterpiece of torture.

The blades did their job, carving him up like a damn Thanksgiving turkey until he was more red than anything else, a broken man barely hanging on to life. But he was stubborn, the fucker, didn't say a word about my father. So, I leaned in real close and whispered with all the venom I possessed, "Should've kept your filthy eyes off my girl. Then maybe, just maybe, you would've walked away from this. But not now." I watched his eyes, the realization dawning that this was the end of the road for him. With one quick motion, I ended it, his life slipping away like darkness at dawn. It was over. Inside the store, I picked out a suit sharp enough to impress Father and a mask that'll keep me a shadow in the crowd. It covers my eyes and my nose but let my mouth free to play with my little bunny later. As I leave the store, suited up with the mask tucked under my arm, I think about Fallon. She's out there, a wild storm wrapped in silk, ready to wreak havoc. Tonight, we aren't just stepping into the darkness; we're diving in headfirst. I hit the gas, the engine's roar drowning out the chaos in my head.

I am stepping out of the car as the valet takes my keys with a nod. I glance back at the sleek lines of the vehicle, a sense that tonight marks more than just another event. Ahead, the museum looms, its grandeur transformed into a den of masquerade and whispers, a place where masks aren't just for show. They hide the facets of truth that claw for air beneath the surface. I make my way up the stone steps.

As I enter the dimly lit foyer, strains of classical music surge around me, a haunting melody that infiltrates my mind, stirring fucking memories I've tried to lock away. Suddenly, I'm nine years old again, holed up in a dark closet, the taste of tears and dust on my lips. The melody from the party outside seeps through the walls, a cruel reminder of the world from which I've been cast aside. And then, the door opens, Daniel, his hand outstretched, pulling me back into the light.

Shaking my head, I try to dispel the ghosts of the past, pulling the present into focus. The chatter of the gathered crowd resonates with a different tone tonight. Masks sit atop every face, half-concealed identities playing at a game where anonymity is the fragile barrier against the reality outside. I muscle through the crowd, feeling the beat of the night pump through my veins. I sense eyes on me, and I know every move I make is under a spotlight. I walk confidently, calculating distances and counting people when I see her.

She's fucking breathtaking; each step she takes is a siren's call I'm helpless to resist. Her dark gown tight on her perfect figure, she looks like the mother of this whole world, the queen of each fucking heart. My gaze fixed on her as she waded through the sea of masked folks as Franco introduced Valentina and her to his people. I drift unseen to the outskirts, content to observe from the darkness, a guardian keeping watch.

Stuck in the damn corner of this fancy-ass museum, the weight of the serpent inked onto my chest anchors me, its coiling presence a constant reminder that danger takes many forms. Sometimes, even your own father. As the event swirls around us, my focus remains on Fallon. The way she navigates the room, an actress on a stage far grander. She's fucking mesmerizing. Tonight, I am both audience and actor in a story where our paths are all tangled up, walking a tightrope together. The masquerade ball is in full swing, and these dolled-up snobs are strutting around, hiding their bullshit behind masks and fake smiles. Everything's a game of show-off, but I ain't here to play nice.

You have to keep an eye on Fallon and make sure none of these greedy vultures get too close. A shadow creeps up on me, and I don't need an introduction to know who it is. I whip my head around, and there's Daniel under that shiny silver mask of his. "You manage to dig up anything good?" I growl, not in the mood for his cryptic shit tonight. He's got that look in his eye, the one that says he's got news. Daniel's quiet for a beat, probably sizing up the risk of whatever he's about to spill. These walls have ears, and you never know which fancy dress is actually a wolf in sheep's clothing.

Finally, he leans in and lowers his voice to near silence, "Franco's shaking hands with the devil right now." He says it like it's some kind of riddle, but I get it. A smirk tugs at my lips because this is the kind of twist that can swing the game in our favor. "Good work." I nod at him. Daniel fades back into the party like he's just another ghost. I look at who my father's speaking to right now, and I take note of the other man, The new distributor.

I tug at the collar of my shirt, feeling the walls closing in. This place, it's a damn minefield, and everyone's dancing on a powder keg. I glance over at Fallon, safe for the moment. She's playing her part, but I see the strength in her pose, the calculations behind those eyes. She isn't just some trophy, that's for damn sure. Every handshake is a loaded gun, and every whisper is a potential death sentence. I perch at the bar, nursing a whisky that's as rough as my mood. There's something fucking gnawing at me, and it's not the burn of the alcohol on its way down. It's been too long since I've felt... anything. Years of nothing, and now Fallon barge into my life, and it's like I'm goddamn Pandora's box cracked open, all these gut-twisting emotions spilling out pisses me off.

I flick my lighter, fire up a smoke, and let the tendrils of vice fill my lungs. Another puff on my cigarette, and these fucking emotions I don't want come crawling into my mind again.

Sixteen years old young man, wild and cornered. Thrashing against restraints, the bodyguards my old man directed on me, grinning like devils. There's Daniel, my supposed ticket out, but the bastard's just standing there, watching me flounder like a fish gasping on dry land. I'm heaving, trying to buck the guys off, when white coats swarm in, one of them jamming a needle deep into my arm. The room tilts, my head lolls, and I'm out, the darkness swallowing me whole.

Back in the present, the whisky's warmth does nothing to chase away the chills from that flashback. Now it's curling back to life, stoked by a girl who's got no business rattling my cage. I take another drag, exhale a smoky sigh, and fix my glare on the liquid amber in my glass. It's time to get my head on straight.

I walk up in Fallon's direction like I own the damn place, which isn't too far from the truth. My goddess, draped in her sleek dress that's got every head turning, is not realizing how fast I'm going to her, talking with guests. She stands next to Franco, who's laying out his charm like a royal carpet for the vultures circling his wealth. Franco and Valentina put on a show, a perfect picture of the power couple. As I stride toward them, Franco's eyes snap to mine, sharp as ever, an unspoken challenge hanging between us. He's the king in his suited armor, but I'm the renegade prince, the serpent in his Eden, and he knows it. Valentina greets me first, a flutter of pleasantries that barely hides the unease ticking in her eyes. She knows all too well the game we're playing, the game I plan to end.

Franco's voice slices the tension, "Why are you here?" Venom drips from each syllable, a reminder of the rift that's grown between us. But I give him no words. My eyes are locked on Fallon, who's watching the scene from the sidelines. I stretch out my hand to her, the gesture simple but seething with the tension that's simmering beneath our skin. "Dance with me?" I ask, and she doesn't even blink. It's dangerous, it's a bad idea, but I need to smell her, touch her, feel her closeness.

Her hand slips into mine, and I lead her away, hungry eyes trailing after us, toward the dance floor where violins cry slow, haunting melodies that echo the rhythm of my heart. The crowd parts for us like we're royalty stepping into our court. The slow violin swells, wrapping around us as I pull her close. Our bodies find a rhythm all their own, a dance of power and rebellion played out under the watching eyes of the world we're about to set on fire.

I've got Fallon right up against me; her warmth and that subtle floral aroma from her skin are keeping me hooked. My hand rests firmly on the small of her back, giving her just enough push to know I'm there. The way she syncs with me, moving like she's born from the rhythm, really gets my heart racing. I lean in, close enough to let my lips brush the shell of her ear. "You're perfect," I murmur. The shudder that ripples through her tells me she's right there with me. A low growl rumbles in my chest, more animal than man, as I breathe her in. Her scent is all over me, taking my senses hostage. What I would give to rip this skin of yours and keep it on me every goddam time.

Her hair tickles my nose, and I can't resist. I bury my face in it, inhaling deeply. "Found the next distributor," I confess, and the satisfaction of dropping that piece of intel doesn't miss its mark. I can feel her mind ticking, the gears turning as the music plays in the background. The secret's out, hanging between us, and with our bodies still moving in tandem, it's a promise of the chaos we'll unleash, her and I.

CHAPTER 30

UNLEASHED

FALLON

As the bright chandeliers cast their gleaming light across the grand ballroom, I find myself swept into the rhythm of a dance. Camden stands before me, his posture a tower of strength, each lean muscle coiled beneath his finery. He leads with a precision that borders on the possessive, his movements so sure and measured they leave no room for doubt or resistance.

I follow, my gown whispering across the polished floor, a whisper that speaks of secrets and silent pledges. Our bodies move in tandem, his frame an immovable presence that guides and commands in equal measure. I look up, seeking a glimpse of the man behind the grey mask, yearning to find his eyes. But he's a fortress, his gaze darting through the crowd, vigilant and cautious, as though every shadow conceals a threat. His alertness is a contrast to the festive air that fills the room. But inside, I'm buzzing with excitement, even if I look calm on the outside.

As we dance, I sense eyes upon us, the pointed glances of my mother and the calculated appraisal of my stepfather, their scrutiny a weight that bears down upon my shoulders. I lean my face close to his neck, my voice barely a whisper above the orchestra's crescendo. "What's next?"

Camden doesn't answer, but his grip on my waist tightens ever so slightly. As the final note quivers into silence, we break apart. Camden gives a curt nod, placing his head in level with mine. "We kill him."

As Camden strides off the dance floor suddenly, my curiosity kicks in. I can't help but watch him, noticing the way his muscles play under his tight shirt with each determined step he takes. There's a tug in my chest, a thread of intrigue pulling me along, even as my feet carry me back to my family. Before I can ponder further, Franco is at my side, "Fallon, I must say you've certainly impressed me this evening. It seems you and Camden are finally on good terms." He observes. Responding with polite neutrality, I nod and murmur an affirmation, hoping to stem any further discussion about Camden.

My gaze drifts once more to the exit, and I catch a glimpse of two figures that shouldn't make sense this close together, Cam and Daniel, slipping through the building's threshold. Puzzlement knits my brows together. What could possibly be drawing those two away together? With a quiet excuse, I disentangle myself from the group and head towards the bathroom needing to collect my toughs.

I retreat to the opulent bathroom, a classy decor of marble and dim lights. Positioning myself before the mirror, I search my reflection in the hope of finding a glimpse of the old Fallon. The one that doesn't know all the shit that haunts the new one.

The door clicks shut again, and before I can see who has entered, I feel him, his powerful presence, overwhelming and intoxicating. His heat radiates against my back, contrasting with the cool stone counter. Without warning, I'm trapped between him and the unyielding surface. A gasp escapes me as Camden's hardness presses into my lower back. "What are you doing here? I saw you going out." I ask, breathless. Camden grabs a handful of my hair, yanking my head back with a calculated aggression that sends a thrilling panic racing through my bloodstream.

His lips crash against mine, an eruption of pent-up need and dark desire. His touch is fire, and I am the kindling, eager and willing to be consumed. As his hand travels down my spine, each vertebra bows to his commanding touch, my body arching to meet every sensation. His eyes, twin storms of blue, capture mine in the mirror. Our reflection melds into a single entity. A shiver cascades down my body. His breath is a whisper against my skin, "What are you doing to me, Fallon?" His voice trails off, the vibration of his words tangling my skin. I don't respond and simply give him my gaze in the mirror. I don't know what to say anyway. "You drive me completely mad, and you mess up my plans every fucking time." He adds.

One of his large hands captures one of my breasts roughly; the sensation of my hardened nipple against the fabric of my dress is almost painful. "I need to punish you for driving me so fucking crazy. Bend over bunny." I can't help but twitch at the faint clacking sound echoing from somewhere in the gallery halls, footsteps approaching. My heart hammers against my ribcage, the fear that the bathroom door might swing open at any second, clawing at my sanity. I catch his reflection in the mirror, his eyes hungry and fixed on me. His hand moves, a blur of motion, and a sharp sting explodes across my backside. I hiss, pain blooming and spreading like wildfire. It's violent and unyielding, a pointed reminder that I'm not in control here, not really. "Listen, Fallon," he commands, his deep voice reverberating off the tiles, "like the good girl I know you can be." His outburst is a wake-up call.

We're not two kids sneaking around; we're in the middle of a deadly serious situation where the stakes are life. The air between us is an electric field, charged and pulsing with an energy that is both threatening and undeniably seductive. My skin is aflame, a riotous mix of anticipation and desire. I pitch forward, my hand bracing against my ankles, as his presence fills the room behind me. I catch the hiss of satisfaction that escapes him as he hoists my dress up to my hips, exposing the secret I'd hidden beneath: my bare skin with no panties. With a swift, decisive movement, Cam drops to his knees. I gasp as his face meets my cunt, his breath a warm promise against my already damp heat. I shiver, feeling his tongue tease my clitoris. He's marking his territory, claiming me in the most primal way. The heat rising in me makes me moan, and he rises, towers over me once again, his words like a brand against my consciousness. "You're playing with fire, coming out without panties." He growls low in his throat, a predator tantalizing his prey. "I'll have to fill you up with my cum now. Have you feel it dripping down your legs after."

I tilt my head back, exposing my throat, the pulse there thunderous under my skin. I want him to see the desire etched on my face, the desperate yearning for him to follow through on his threat. He's right; this is naughty and dangerous. I knew it when I chose to forgo the underwear, a silent invitation to this very moment. Now, I'm ready to reap the wicked reward, to let the sensation of his claiming to linger as a visceral reminder of our entanglement. He forcefully spreads my legs. My instinct is to stand, to say no, but Camden shoves my face back down, my head between my knees. His rough voice cuts the air, tinged with mockery, "Fuck it. You want to play the victim, little bunny?" Frozen, I don't make a sound. I'm all exposed to him, spread wide, a display of vulnerability and provocation. Without warning, he spanks me hard, right on my pussy. I squeal in pain, the sharp sting drawing a veil of tears to my eyes. His laughter echoes through the bathroom, a cruel note that reverberates against the walls and within my skull. "Remember, Fallon," he sneers, his presence a looming threat, "if you do not use the safe word, I'll continue." The power to stop this, the urge to say the word hangs on the edge of my lips, but silence takes over. Am I paralyzed by fear, or is it the allure of the darkness beckoning me further?   Muscles quivering and breaths escaping in ragged whispers, the marble of the museum bathroom is cold and unyielding against my palms, but the heat between us is a relentless inferno. Cam enters me with a force that borders on reckless. Each thrust is punishing. His powerful hands, unyielding, grasping my hips, guiding me back onto him with a carnal rhythm that robs me of my senses. I am nothing but a vessel of desire, writhing under his command. His fingers, calloused and demanding, find one of my nipples, pinching it hard enough to make me gasp. The sharp jolt of pleasure-pain shoots directly to my core, amplifying the pleasure.

His voice is a coarse melody in my ear, dripping with sinful promises and commands that stir the darkest depths of my being. "That's it, Fallon," he growls, his voice a blade cutting through the heavy air. "Take it. Take every fucking inch." The sensation of being completely filled, of being owned by this man, my stepbrother, is both overwhelming and intoxicating. His words are filthy, yet they are exactly what I crave. Camden senses my nearness to the edge, the clenching of my inner walls betraying my impending release. "You're gonna come for me, Fallon," he commands, his voice a dangerous tone that sends shivers down my spine. "I want to feel you squeeze my cock with that tight pussy." I am spiraling, losing myself to his dominance, to the relentless pounding that pushes me toward oblivion. "Please, Cam," I beg, my voice a desperate plea lost in the cacophony of our bodies slapping together. "Come now, Fallon!" he orders, and I obey, my body convulsing around him in uncontrollable spasms. As the waves of pleasure subside, I'm left panting, his hands the only thing keeping me from collapsing. With a final, brutal thrust, I shatter, my climax ripping through me like lightning. Camden's hands grip me tighter, his own release heralded by a low grunt as he buries himself deep within me, marking me with his cum. Camden's heavy breaths fan the damp hair at my nape. He leans closer, his lips brushing against my ear. "There's no turning back for you, bunny." We remain entangled, the afterglow enveloping us as we brace for the shit beyond these walls.

CHAPTER 31

TRAINING WITH A GOD

FALLON

The world outside blurs into streaks of darkness, illuminated by occasional flashes of streetlights as Camden's car cuts through the night. My heart races with each passing second, the heavy silence in the car punctuated only by the growl of the engine, a beast on the prowl, much like the man behind the wheel. I steal a glance at Cam, his profile stark against the fleeting lights.

The tension in his jaw suggests that his thoughts are as tumultuous as mine. We're in this together, bound by a mission that's grown bigger than either of us. "So, what's the plan?" I ask, my voice steady despite the storm of emotions churning within me. I need to know more to understand what we're diving into. His eyes flash my way, their depths unreadable. "We hack into Franco's network, find the location of the distributor, kill him, and free the people in the container." I nod, the weight of our task settling on my shoulders. It's a dangerous mission we're about to step into, one where any misstep could be fatal. "I can't wrap my head around the fact that you've been doing this forever. It must be really hard to carry this as a burden." I honestly say. His big hand, full of scars, rests on my thigh, and the other stays on the steering wheel. "I'm sorry for you, Cam," I add. His fingers tighten against my skin, and I can see on his face the tension appearing in the corner of his mouth. But still, he's magnificent, truly a god. His beard of a few days accentuates his strong features, and a ton of questions invade me. A realization that I don't know a lot about him. I know him, but not his soul. I know he has one somewhere behind the monster. "Why did I see you talking and leaving with Daniel the other day at the ball?" He turns his head towards me for a few seconds and looks into mine. His thumb delicately grazed my knee. "Daniel is on my side. He always has been. He's been working for my dad for as long as I can remember. When my father was beating me, letting his friends tie me up on a chair in the middle of the living room and use me as a punching bag when he locked me in a closet for hours when he drugged me. Daniel was always the one who came in and got me out of the situation. "

I try to chase away the tears that flood the corners of my eyes, but Camden, glancing at my face, catches a glimpse of them. "Fuck it. Don't cry, baby. It's been a long time, and now I have the most beautiful goddess to take revenge with me." Yet the thought of him young, suffering fuels a fire in me that's equal parts rage and sadness. I'll burn everything to the ground if it means keeping this grown-ass man safe.

The plan we developed during the last few days is simple in theory: spy, attack at the right moment, and free the people. Franco's containers at the port are fortified and guarded by layers of security, and after the masked ball, Cam and Daniel made maps and counts of them so we're prepared. Our chances are slim, but the thought of those poor, enslaved, and exploited children and women hardens my resolve. "But first, I'll train you," Camden says. His hands tighten on the steering wheel, his determination palpable. "I've been preparing for this for a long time, Fallon. But you, even tho I'm pretty impressed with your capability, need a bit more precision." The fierce certainty in his voice sends a shiver down my spine. I'm about to respond when he suddenly swerves onto a less-traveled road, the car's tires crunching on the gravel underneath.

We're heading into the deserted warehouse district. The car comes to a jolting stop, and Cam turns to me, his voice slicing with a sharpness I've never heard before. "Fuck, you're the prettiest death these fuckers could have dreamed." He leans in, so close, his lips barely touching mine.

As the last echo of the slammed door fades into silence, he guides me through the night, his car a shadow that swallows the deserted street. His secret cache is just ahead, and my breath comes quick with anticipation. We come to a halt in front of what seems like an abandoned shop, its windows boarded up, the neon sign above us flickering weakly.

This is it, Camden's secret armory, a place where light doesn't dare to tread. "What, no breadcrumbs to find your way back, Cam?" My voice is high, trying to make the atmosphere less heavy with my dumb-ass joke, but he just smirks, that infuriating smirk that does things to me I don't want to admit. With his perfect fucking smile. He seems so normal.

He pulls me in, and a chill runs down my spine as the door shuts behind us, throwing us into almost total darkness. As my eyes get used to it, I look around, seeing all sorts of weapons hanging on the walls. Guns, knives, everything you'd need to make it in a world where you've got to fend for yourself. And there it is his thoughtful touch in the middle of all this madness. A tidy stack of sports bras and leggings, clearly picked out with care, most likely by him, just for me. It throws me for a loop, a hint of warmth spreading inside me. Camden, with his psycho exterior, has a kind side that's oddly captivating. "Nice touch with the gear," I say, unable to hide the surprise in my voice. He shrugs, a faint smile dancing on his lips.

We don't waste time. He's all business, and I fall into step. He's got me learning the curves and lines of a handgun, the cold metal a strange extension of my hand. I'm a quick study, my focus laser sharp as I aim down the sight, feeling the power at my fingertips, the seductive promise of control. Camden observes with a piercing stare. As our hands touch, when he hands me a knife, a jolt of heat rushes through me. The tension between us has nothing to do with the arsenal nearby. It's a magnetic pull we both feel but won't admit to each other with clear words.

The training is tough, stretching me to the edge. I'm drenched in sweat, catching my breath, the sports bra sticking to me. It's an intense work of moves and blocks, and Camden doesn't let up, pushing me to go further, quicker. We're battling invisible foes, gearing up for a conflict I never asked for. His hand grips mine, correcting my stance, and our eyes lock. It's electric, this thing between us, and I'm drowning in the depths of his blue gaze. The air is ripe with something dark and forbidden. He leans in close, too close, his breath a whisper against my ear as he speaks, each word laced with a challenge. "Don't think this makes you safe, Fallon. Weapons are just tools. Survival? That's a state of mind."And just like that, we're back in the thick of it. I'm mastering shots, blows, and hand-to-hand combat. Yet, underneath the grit, the weaponry, and the urgent need to survive, there's this spark. That mysterious attraction that keeps pulling me toward him, making me ponder what could happen if I fully embrace it... My muscles scream, my lungs burn, and the air in the training room is thick and heavy. Camden's there, all focus and fury, pushing me past the brink.

He demands perfection; we're talking life and death, and my every instinct shouts to meet his challenge. But his lessons have this crazy edge to them, a thrill that's both exciting and scary. We're really close, maybe too close, with his warmth mixing with the cold steel of the blade I'm holding, this sleek, dangerous thing that's starting to feel like it's just a part of me. "Focus, Fallon," he barks, a command that sends adrenaline surging through my veins. The room is our coliseum, and I can almost hear the crowd baying for blood. Camden's staring me down, and he totally gets it. He sees the fire in my moves, the wildness in my defense. I'm backed against the wall, but it's not about giving in. It's this raw need to take charge, to own the space between us. He's throwing down a challenge with each move, and man, I'm so ready to flip the script. He closes in, and the space between us crackles with something wild and dangerous. Sweat beads at my temple, but it's not exhaustion. It's the thrill of the hunt, the electricity of impending conquest. "Come on, Fallon," he snarls. His breath fans my face, hot and heavy with the scent of man and might.

I lunge, the blade slicing the air with a hiss, a strike meant to disarm, to unnerve. He sidesteps, a grin curling his lips, a demonic, honest smile of pleasure that tells me he's enjoying this far too much. My leg swings out, a desperate attempt to bring him down, but he's immovable, a pillar of strength against my storm. We crash together like waves hitting a cliff, and there's this intense moment where we're all tangled up. His hands on me are a weird blend, neither rough nor soft, adding to the rising tension between us. "Always so eager to prove yourself," he murmurs, voice thick with something unspoken. I'm breathing hard. Each inhale laced with the musk of his skin, the tantalizing nearness of him. The blade feels slick in my sweaty grip, but it's the heat of his stare that truly unsettles me, an inferno that threatens to consume my resolve. "Get off," I manage, my voice a raspy order that betrays the chaos he stirs within me. But he doesn't listen, his weight a declaration, his breath a caress of danger on my skin.

The vibe in the air is all about pain, hints of pleasure, and this crazy tug-of-war right in between. We're teetering on the edge, going all out. Our physical showdown says way more than any talk could. It's like a back-and-forth, all happening while death keeps an eye on us. "You play a dangerous game," he whispers, and the menace in his voice is a spark that ignites the tension, wrapping us in a cocoon of forbidden fire.

The boundary between ally and adversary fades, like a stain on paper marking either our downfall or our fate. As we face each other, taking in the moment, it hits me: the intense clash between us, a mix of raw attraction and survival instincts that could tear us apart.

CHAPTER 32

IS THIS LOVE?

CAMDEN

The urge to take her, to punish her for making my life revolve around her, has gone through me far too often this past week. But I didn't succumb. We had work and shit to do. She tried, at every training session, to stick her little ass on my cock, to look at me like she wanted to eat me alive. But we have to stay focused. Her progress was almost immediate as if she was born to become a killing machine. Fuck, if this doesn't make me fall ever more in love. Love, what a weird word. I often think about it during my long, sleepless nights. I think the idea that her dying would feel like my own end shows just how much I love her.

Every day, as soon as the sun rises, we leave the manor in silence; Daniel will give us a cover story if anyone asks questions. We come to train until the rays of light disappear to give way to the night. I brought her back and watched her disappear into her room in silence. It's disappointing, I know, bunny, I too want to keep you, tied to the foot of my bed, in a fucking cage if I have to. But not right now. Once this shit show is over, we will be able to play as we want.

The evening unfolds like many others, with me in front of my screens, a whiskey in one hand and a cigarette in the other. I gaze at my woman, peacefully asleep in her bed. What the fuck did I do in this fucked up world to deserve her? I don't know. And I don't care. My phone buzzes, and I pick it up, answering without checking the caller ID. "Why are you dragging her into this Camden?" Daniel's voice is upset, and it makes me sigh. "Why don't you go wash a car or something? That's what you do when I piss you off, uh?"

"You'll get her killed." I press the bridge of my nose, annoyed. "Daniel. I'll never let someone kill her. Not even touch her. Be assured about that."

"I really hope this is true. Because your psycho ass doesn't really matter to me anymore." He's lying. I know he sees me like his own son. Always has. It makes me smile. "Camden, when are you planning on going to the port?" I stand up, shut off the screen, and head to the bathroom to hop in the shower. "Their meeting is Monday night. So, use your brain, big guy." I turn on the water, and it starts to fill the space with hot mist. "I want to be there for her." He speaks. "No. This is my fucking revenge. And I want to savor it with MY fucking woman.
"

"You are really something else." "Goodnight, Daniel." I hang up and drop the phone on top of the countertop. Fuck if he's annoying. Always has been. But if he had not been here, I would be dead by now. The steam swirls around me, all-consuming, a dense fog that seems to cling to my skin. The water's hot as the devil's ass, my own private inferno right here in the chrome and glass confines of my shower. And my body wastes no time; I'm hard, so fucking hard, my hand wrapped around my length as I stroke, rough and punishing. My knuckles go white as I grip myself tighter, every pump a tease to my flesh. The slick sound of my hand moving over my cock echoes off the tiles, blending with the relentless drum of water from above. I'm not gentle, not delicate, I'm a fucking animal, and this, this is what I need.

With each vicious tug, each twist of my wrist, I'm teetering on the cliff's edge, dangling over the precipice of release. I bite back a groan, clenching my teeth, biting the inside of my cheeks so hard I pierced the skin, the metallic taste of blood filling my mouth and mixing with my saliva. A masochist reveling in the exquisite torture of my own doing. The fantasy that's got me by the balls, it's dark and twisted, but fuck me, it's potent. Fallon, that little vixen, squirming beneath me, her tits bouncing as I plow into her. Would she beg for it? Would she fight? Either way, she'd be mine, and the thought alone drives me to the brink. I slap my palm against the wet tile, my movements growing frenetic. Yeah, I'm vile, nasty even, but at this moment, I'm free. I lean into the pain, want to feel that sting, that bite on my skin, a fucking reminder that I'm alive. My breaths come in ragged gasps, the pent-up lust and aggression melding into this raw, fierce rhythm that's got me hooked. And as the surge builds, catapulting me toward that peak, I can't hold back. With a shuddering breath and a guttural curse, I come undone, spilling my cum in a hot rush, the release a fucking exorcism of every pent-up frustration within me. Each pulse of my cock milks me dry, my vision going white with the sheer force of it.

And as I pant there, water and release dripping down my flesh, I realize that Fallon's under my skin now, a depraved obsession I will never be able to shake.

I jolt awake, every damn sense on high alert. Growing up in constant fear teaches you to stay sharp even in your sleep. Just as my eyes snap open, someone's hovering over me. Without thinking, I grab them by the shoulders and slam them down, pinning them with my knee in the pitch-black darkness. "You fucker." I reach over to my bedside table and flick on the small lamp. Its soft light fills the room, revealing the space, and I quickly let go of the intruder. "The fuck you are doing here, bunny. Are you all right?" Concern seizes my face; I can sense my brows creased together." My bad. She blows between two puffs of air.

She stands up, and it allows my eyes to see her body in panties with just a little night camisole; she is a dream. "I couldn't sleep. I had nightmares. I... I wanted to come and see you." I pull back, a wave of worry hitting me. Is this typical? Why is she seeking comfort from a living nightmare?

Before I know it, my hands act on their own, reaching out to her instantly. I grasp the back of her head, run my fingers through her golden hair, and pull her close to my chest. I take in her scent for a moment. "Come in bed with me." I've never slept with anyone other than my demons, but right now, my bunny needs me. I lay back, and she quickly settled next to me, placing her upper body on my chest. I shut my eyes, aiming to drift back to sleep. Tomorrow's the final day before our major move, and there are still a few tasks, purchases, and checks left on my list. "Do you want to tell me about the harm Franco has done to you? You slipped me a word about it, but it was very vague." Her voice is soft and full of care.

I grunt softly. "Not now." She doesn't insist. Instead, she lets one of her hands caress my bare belly. Draw small circles along my abs. "Do you want to tell me about your nightmares?" I whisper. "It's blurry; there were children screaming for help. I saw a pregnant woman being raped and opened to snatch her baby from her." I can hear the grimace in her voice. "Then I saw myself as a child, thin, hungry. Sitting in a living room, I think it was one of the shabby apartments Valentina rented when I was young. A man sitting next to me, well dressed, talking with my mother. Then I'd see him touch my thigh." I'm fucking boiling. "Did he rape you?" Her hands stop the motion, her voice filled with sadness. "I don't know. I don't remember." I'll need to know. If someone hurt her when she was just a kid, he deserves all hell falling on his death. I kiss her hair and place my arms around her. "Now, sleep before I tie you up and destroy your ass." "And if that's what I want." "That's not what you need. Sleep, bunny." I've firmly decided that I want to start each day with Fallon's legs, arms, and hair wrapped around me like right now. The real challenge? Getting out of bed without disturbing her. She doesn't have to come with me to get around, sitting in my car today. So, I want to let her sleep as much as she needs. When I'm finally able to get myself out of her arms and ready to go, I reach for my phone and shoot her a text for when she eventually wakes up.

Left for the day to watch and monitor the port. Stay home. Don't die. And don't touch that damn plastic dick.

CHAPTER 33

BYE MOM

FALLON

I step into the big dining room with a sense of ease; spending the night with Camden truly refreshed me. Nestled close to him felt comforting, and waking up to find the bed cold and vacant made me instinctively check my phone. As anticipated, there was a message waiting for me. I understand. I know it's essential, but I wish I could have done that with him.

"Good morning, Fallon." Franco's voice snaps me

out of my thoughts, and I sit down to his left. "Good morning." I nod in his direction and smile with my lips in a thin line as I looked at my mother. "Friday, I'm going to need your help, my beautiful daughter. I am organizing an event here at the house; we'll receive clients and friends and talk business. I'd love for you to cover the event for our social media." He finishes his sentence with a sip of his coffee, and I don't know if it's the fact he called me his beautiful daughter or that his face seems happy that took me out.

This asshole, I look at him with the best mask of innocence I'm able to put on. But I know that by Friday, he's going to be dead. "It'll make me happy to assist." He shoots me a smile. The morning sun sneaks through the drapes, giving the dining room a cozy vibe. As I mix the cream into my coffee, I pick up on Franco's uneasy vibe when he stands up abruptly, muttering something about having to go.

Once he's gone, the room feels emptier, the air

between me and my mother thick with unspoken words. She sits across from me, her elegance unaffected by the early hour, and yet there's a softness in her eyes today that I seldom see. "Mom," I begin, pausing just briefly before speaking again. "Do you really know Franco?"

Our eyes lock, and I catch a glimpse of something profound, a mutual acknowledgment of the facades we put on. "Yes, Fallon," she replies, her voice smooth as silk. "I know him." I can't shake the feeling of discomfort, the sensation of treading on the edge of something dark and troubling. Yet, I push those concerns aside, reaching for something, anything, that might feel normal, even if just for a moment. "What's your plan for Monday night?" I probe, my curiosity tinged with a genuine concern for her well-being. She grins, but there's a hint of distance in her eyes, mentioning a dinner with her new crew of girlfriends, just another social event in her meticulously planned world.

I know these dinners, full of laughter and clinking

glasses, are just a veneer over the loneliness that I sense in her. An idea suddenly takes hold of me, and before I can second-guess myself, I blurt out the invitation. "Why don't we go shopping? You and me?" Shopping is her guilty pleasure.

My mom's taken aback, her eyes briefly widening before she gives a real smile. The idea warms my heart; just the thought of us hanging out like that feels so genuine and special. And as I sit there, watching her reaction, I'm struck by the realization that this might be our last normal morning.

I hide the tremble in my hands as I lift the coffee cup to my lips, the steam warm against my skin. In this brief instant, I grasp the delicate bond I share with my mother. It's a glimmer of hope amid encroaching darkness, reminding me of the ordinary life I'm striving to maintain for both of us.

The rain taps a consistent beat on the car's roof, its rhythm matching the quietness between my mom and me. As we make our way into town, I wrap my arms around myself, attempting to ward off the chill sneaking in, even with the heater on. "You ready for our girl day shopping, Fallon?" Mom's gentle voice cuts through the quiet, pulling me from my thoughts. I nod, words escaping me. Encased in the car's interior, we move forward, with the rhythmic sound of the windshield wipers and sporadic sighs from Mom filling the space between us. The silence stretches, taut and uneasy. I sense her glances, heavy with unasked questions. I brace myself for the inevitable, the probing into my life, into Camden. Finally, it comes casual yet loaded. "Fallon, what's going on with you and Camden?"

A warmth rises in my neck, and I divert my eyes to the rain-soaked scenery outside. Denial becomes my immediate refuge, hastily thrown up. "Nothing's going on, Valentina."

"I'm not blind, sweetheart. I see the way you two are with each other." The car is suddenly suffocating, the weight of truth pressing against my chest. I can't bring myself to confirm her suspicions, to admit the connection with Camden. "You're wrong," is all I manage, my voice a mere whisper against the drumming rain. Her response is soft, "Sweetie, I'm rarely wrong about these things." The town looms ahead. Daniel parks by the curb, the engine's hum silenced as he turns off the car.

We sit there a moment longer, the world outside a monochrome of grey and the echo of raindrops, a baptism, a cleansing, perhaps, of the secrets that cling to my skin.

Stepping into the rain, each droplet feels like a cold embrace against my skin as we navigate through the town's core. The shift in surroundings doesn't lighten the dense atmosphere, nor does it diminish the weight of my mom's words.

I'm looking in the rows of clothes when a lingerie set catches my eye further into the store. A laced, black, sheer lace top with a metal ring just above the chest. The panties, also black, made of lace, are naughty, without fla

fla, just beautiful. I take it all and head to one of the fitting rooms. Once inside, I hurriedly take off my soaked clothes sticking to my skin and put on the lingerie. My fingers trace the elastic of the panties before sliding up my belly, between my breasts, to finish on my throat. Opening the palm of my hand, I tighten the grip around my neck. Tucked away in the sanctuary of the changing room that smells faintly of perfume and new fabric. The mirror reflects my image back at me, the black dentelle of the lingerie set clinging to my skin. It's more than just clothing; it's a statement of power, seduction, and sexiness.

A wicked idea takes shape, and I snap a photo before I can second-guess it. One hand provocatively dipped into the front of the panties, the other at my throat. My fingers hesitate for a mere moment before I hit send. The thought of his reaction, a mix of desire and perhaps anger, sends a thrill spiraling through me, and I giggle like a schoolgirl. Either way, the vision of his self-control unraveling is intoxicating.

The city's buzz is like a distant song playing as I

feel a bit daring. I carefully slip off the fancy lingerie, making sure not to mess up the pretty lace, and the room's cool air gives me a chill. I'm totally tuned into everything around me. I dashed to the checkout. Yep, I'm grabbing that for sure. Goodies paid, mom in check with her unbelievable amount of bags. We left the store, the little bag with my new purchase, a tantalizing secret against my side. My phone buzzes, signaling his reply is already there. The message icon pops up, and I feel a rush of anticipation. I hesitate before tapping it. His words light up the screen.

I told you to stay home. First mistake.

Second mistake was sending me such a sexy photo when I'm so far away.

Buy me a new belt. I need one.

You're beautiful. Like the fucking goddess, you are bunny.

When my eyes come up from my phone, it's the faces of Valentina and Daniel waiting for me, confused, that greet me. "Who makes you smile like that, Fallon." Her question seems honest and full of goodwill. "No one. Stop fucking snooping in my shit." She shrugs, accustomed to my

mood swings with her. We've never really had a great relationship, and I think that's starting to weigh on me. She's my mom. "Do you love me? Mom." The look of horror that painted her face when we sat in the car almost made me feel bad. "What the fuck Fallon. YES, I love you." I tilt my head and squint, trying to analyze her answer.

"Why don't I remember my childhood? Why am I so fucked?" She turns her head and looks out the window. Ah. Here's the Valentina I know. Unable to own up to her mistakes or even to be honest with me. "That's what I taught," I whisper, grabbing my phone again and sending a quick message to Cam.

Can't wait to see you.

Tonight. I'll come pick you up in your room when I come back.

I smile and put it in my jacket pocket before moving my body forward to the front of the vehicle between the benches. "Please, Daniel, stop at the next superstore you find. I need to buy a belt."

CHAPTER 34

WAKE UP BUNNY

CAMDEN

After a long day of following my new target, Roman Beau, I'm fucking tired. This man is the cliché of the shady businessman. Obese, his wife, seems to be sixteen years old, full of flamboyant jewelry, and above all, easy to spot. I now have a good idea of how fast he moves, how many guards are left with him, four. For the first time since I decided Fallon was mine, I realized what really awaits us tomorrow. I've always known that the chance of me coming out of this vendetta alive was half, but now that she's part of the equation, I can't afford to fail. And if she falls, I fall with her.

Opening the damn door that Fallon crossed for the first time weeks ago, I make my way, like the shadow I am, to her bedroom door. Sneaking around Fallon's room, the nighttime quietness kind of wraps around me. I see her chest moving gently as she breathes and notice how peaceful she looks sleeping, considering the shit that's been our lives. It could be the last time I watch her like this. It's a thought that grips me, a fist around my heart, squeezing without mercy.

Tonight's different. Tonight, I want her to pray to me like I'm her God. And in the same breath, I'm gonna worship her like the deity she's been all along. But before I claim her once more, my gaze lands on a little white paper bag adorned with loopy handwriting: "For Cam." There's something oddly loving about this. A chuckle breaks free from my lips. Inside, the soft feel of leather greets my fingers, the new belt. Fucking perfect. The covers fall away at my touch, revealing the silhouette of her body. Her skin, hugged by that sinful lingerie, sends a surge of lust straight to my groin. I scoop her up easily, her body light in my arms. She doesn't stir, her slumber as deep as the secret that binds us. I'm carrying her, the contents of the bag clutched in my other hand, and we set off toward my room.

My footsteps are quiet, a predator's grace, and I can't help the smirk that feathers across my face. I'm about to lay her down on my bed and start the worship I've been dying for all this goddamn time. Because if this is our last night on this earth together, I'll be damned if I don't leave her with a taste of heaven.

The silence of the night wraps around me, thick and heavy, as I sit, watching Fallon. Her soft exhales are a rhythmic lullaby, fleeting signs of tranquil slumber I dare not disturb. She's sprawled across my bed, a mess of limbs and tousled hair. Carefully, I pick up the new belt I'd been eyeing, the leather smooth and cool in my hands. A sinister smile plays on my lips as I loop it gently, meticulously, around her delicate neck. The symbolism isn't lost on me. She's mine to control, mine to dominate. I seat myself between her thighs, my tongue tracing the soft lines of her belly, savoring the warmth of her skin while my mind races with all the unspeakable things I'm about to do. I work my way down, lips planting feverish kisses on the inside of her thighs, my palm gliding over the thin fabric of her panties. My fingers teased her pussy through the thin tissue barrier, feeling the heat and wetness beginning to form. A flutter of pride stirs in me. She's responding even in her sleep, her body betraying her with every shiver and quiet moan.

Finally, she stirs, her movements lazy and slow, the soft sounds of her pleasure soon turning to confusion. Her eyes snap open wide with panic, a bunny realizing it's trapped. It's beautiful, this moment of pure fear. I silence her panic with gentle kisses, my lips softly pressing against hers, shushing, soothing. "Shhh, it's just me," I whisper against her mouth. Her eyes, once wild with fright, glaze over with recognition and then a dawning calm. She knows she's safe, or as safe as one can be in the arms of a viper like me. I lean in close, my voice a low, dangerous purr, reminding her of her earlier disobedience. "You didn't listen, did you, Fallon? Going out today. You need to be taught a lesson. If you're a good girl, you'll get a proper treat." The words are a promise. I rise up and pull her upright with a sharp yank on the belt, tightening it enough to make her gasp, her eyes closing shut with exquisite pressure. "That's it, moan for me, Fallon. Let me hear how much you want it." Commanding her to get on her back, head dangling off the bed, I fucking love the view of her. Her vulnerability is intoxicating, and the trust she places in me is overwhelming. It warms the darkest parts of my soul. I remove my pants, looking her in the eyes. Those fucking honey eyes of hers, begging me to fuck her skull. I trust one time, and my dick is in her mouth; the sight of it bumping, literally, on her throat is something straight out perfect. This view of her upside down, a picture of depraved beauty with my cock sliding between her parted lips.

I tighten the belt around her neck, cutting off her oxygen, watching her struggle, watching her fight for every bit of air, choking on my dick. When she's teetering on the edge of unconsciousness, eyes rolling back, I ease the pressure, allowing her a precious gulp of life. It's a dangerous game, one we both crave, the feeling between breath and suffocation, life and death. I do it again and again, each cycle more intense than the last, her drool coating my cock and her face, her eyes watering in a mix of pleasure and distress. "Good fucking girl," I growl, my praise as filthy as the act itself. "Taking me like you were made for it." She's a vision, the kind of fucked-up perfection that I never knew I needed. And every twist of her lips around me, every guttural noise she makes, it pushes me closer to the edge. Her name reverberates through the room, a sacred mantra as I plunge deeper into her welcoming heat. "Fallon..." God, it's nearly a cry, thick with the need that's wracked my body. On the precipice, my release teetering just at the brink, I pull back. My cock exits her mouth with a pop, leaving us both gasping, me with the sting of denied climax, her with the rawness of being used.

I slap her, and she's all drool and tears, a ruined angel splayed before me, and fuck if the sight doesn't burn right through me. The impact of my hand against her cheek is minimal, a warning, a caress. "Good girl," I whisper.

My next command is immediate and rough. "Now, touch yourself, Fallon." Her obedience is instantaneous, a beauty in submission that takes my fucking breath away. "You're beautiful," I tell her, unapologetically, because she needs to know it, needs to feel it. I'm stroking myself, slow and agonizing, my gaze never leaving her as she pleasures herself for me. "You want me to bleed for you, don't you?" I ask. Her nod, shy and eager, makes me moan. I toss her the small blade from my drawer, my own pulse hammering in anticipation. She positions herself on her knees on top of the bed, the handle sliding between her thighs. Starting to grind it like it's my cock. Fuck me. That's unexpected.

Watching her, I stroke harder, faster, the sight of her riding on cold steel enough to push me to the brink. The room's charged with our filthy needs. And when she comes, I'm there, mouth latching onto her, wanting, no, needing, to taste the breath of her orgasm.

CHAPTER 35

SAVAGE

FALLON

The aftermath sends shivers down my spine as I slowly come back to the world, the tremors of pleasure still echoing through me. Camden's lips trail fire on my neck, hungry, kissing me while I catch my damn breath. I'm awake now, more awake than I've ever been, and it's all because of this man, this half-god, half-devil who kisses me like he's been dying of thirst, and I'm the only damn water for miles.

Suddenly, I'm in motion, yanking Camden by the throat, flipping our positions as he lands beneath me with a heavy 'oomph.' He laughs, the sound rough around the edges, and he's looking at me with eyes that say, 'Bring it on.' "Shirt off. Now!" I command, my voice dripping with authority I didn't even know I had, and he's quick to comply, tearing the fabric off like it's nothing. The sight of him, all muscles and inked skin, has my core clenching again. God, he's a fucking masterpiece. I can't help but admire the view, his erection standing proud and clearly painfully hard. It's like a damn monument to every filthy thought I've ever had, and I want to worship at its base until I know every inch of it by heart. Leaning down on top of him, I whisper, my lips barely brushing against his ear. "Want me to make you come, baby?" He shudders beneath me, and I can feel that huge cock twitch in anticipation. But teasing is a game I excel at, and I'm not about to let him off easy. I roll my hips, a sinuous promise of what's to come, and the world narrows down to just us, two beings consumed by a wild, dangerous hunger. I take the belt from around my neck, snapping it against his chest hard enough to draw a growl from him. "You into this, Camden? You like a little pain with your pleasure?" I ask, my voice laced with dark curiosity. He looks at me, pure sin etched into every line of his face, and says, "Only with you, Fallon. Only with you."

We kiss again, tongue and teeth and everything messy in between. It's a kiss that says 'I love you' without having to say the words, but I whisper them anyway because I can't hold them back anymore. They spill out from my lips on a breath. "I love you." Confusion flickers in his eyes for a split second before they harden once more. Before he can respond, I slide the blade under his chin, just enough to draw a thin line of blood. Licking the wounds with fucking lust, the taste of power intoxicating, I show him his own blood on my tongue. His reaction is feral; grabbing me like a savage, he flips our bodies once more and impales himself inside me with a fierceness that borders on torture. And right there, with every hard thrust, with every desperate moan, we lose ourselves in the storm. Two lost souls finding salvation in each other's arms, even if it's just for this moment, even if it's just for tonight.

The sound of our rough fuck fills the room, echoing back to us from the walls. It's a symphony of gasps, groans, cries, and wet slaps of skin against skin. Under me, Camden is an inexorable force. He flips me, and we roll down the bed, my back hitting the ground hard.

Blood from his throat drips on me, the sticky warmth seeping into my hair, joining the sweat that glues us together. Camden's hands are on me, around me, inside me, everywhere. They brand me with ownership. His grip is fierce on my flesh as he drives into me with ruthless precision. I hate him. I hate the way I now love him, the way he's twisted my desires and made them bow to his will. My head is thrown back, my throat bared, and I feel him there, at the apex of my vulnerability, his teeth grazing the tender skin. "Beg for it," he commands, his voice a harsh whisper that sends a shiver down my spine. There's a pause, a drawn-out moment where the only sound is our labored breathing and the incessant drip of blood from his throat, our perverse lubricant.

In this masochistic tango, we're entwined in the

most intimate of dances, one that's going to end in scars, physical for him, emotional for me. I'm spiraling, every nerve ending on fire as he takes me to the edge and holds me there, teetering on the brink of release. "Please, Cam." Our movements are frantic, unhinged as if we could outrun our demons if only we fuck hard enough, deep enough.

He looks at me, and our eyes connect; I see playfulness in them. He stops his hips movement and brings one of his thumbs to my mouth, pushing it inside; I close my lips around it and suck it. With a grunt, he pulls it out and shoves it into my ass. A little silent scream escapes me, but he starts to move again, the pleasure invading me. My whole body is shivering. I feel it building, that tidal wave of ecstasy that's going to crash over me. I meet him thrust for thrust, matching his ferocity with my own wild abandon.

And when we come, it's together, a cataclysmic event that shakes the foundation of our very beings. Our cries mingle, a duet of passion and pain that seals our fates. We're sticky with sweat and blood and come a tangled mess of limbs. Camden and I catch our breath, both gasping like we just ran a crazy race, our hearts trying to win some unreachable prize.

In the aftermath, there's a silence that screams louder than any moan or slap of flesh. It hangs heavy, suffocating in its intensity. We're just two broken halves of a whole, bound forever now. As I turn to face him, his blue eyes meet mine, the untamed ferocity within them finding its echo in my own gaze. "Let me take you in the bath, baby." He speaks. And I nod.

The warm water feels like a safe haven. Camden's right behind me, both of us soaking in the tub, the steam making our features a bit hazy. It's like he's a magnet, pulling me close without even trying. I lean back into him, curious about what's on his mind. What thoughts are swirling in his mind?

He cleanses both of us with a tenderness that's almost sacred. His touches gentle in their thoroughness. There's a kind of solemnity in the act, a quiet acknowledgment of our shared vulnerabilities. The water swirls around us, carrying away the grime and the blood. We're still, so very still, as if movement might break whatever thing we're building here in this steam-filled cocoon. I close my eyes, and the world narrows down to the sensation of the warmth of Camden's body against mine and the sound of our synchronized breathing.

I've never felt anything like this, a tranquility that's as deep as it is alarming. It's a peace I'm not sure I deserve, but right now, I'm too tired to care. The silence stretches on, filled with a poignant intimacy that's new and delicate, like the first frost on autumn leaves. And as I let out a breath, I didn't realize I'd been holding, I feel myself slipping away, my consciousness edging towards the precipice of sleep.

Not a lot of people, I'm sure, would be able to sleep with this man in the same room and feel secure. But I trust him. I trust him to keep me safe here in the water, here in the world beyond. As I slowly succumb to the pull of fatigue, the last thing I feel is Camden's lips pressing a soft, barely there, kiss to the crown of my head. I fall asleep, tangled up in him, in a bath that's slowly cooling.

CHAPTER 36

GOOD MORNING SUNSHINE

FALLON

The soft light of dawn creeps through the room, casting a warm, gentle glow across the space when I awaken, nestled in a mess of sheets with the comforting warmth of our bodies touching. The reassuring pressure of Camden's arm around me. I hang out there for a bit, digging the steady up-and-down of his chest and feeling his heart thumping under my hand. He's all warm, which feels awesome against the cool morning breeze sneaking in from the cracked window. I carefully plan my move to get out of bed, trying not to disturb the quiet. I gently pull away from our night-long embrace, moving quietly across the bed. As I create a little space between us, I take one more look. He's still asleep, peacefully breathing in a steady rhythm, his skin softly lit by the early morning light.

With soft steps, I sneak out of the cozy spot we made during the night. It's time to face the day and, more importantly, gear up for that big talk with my mom before all hell breaks loose.

As I move quietly through the massive, quiet halls of this mansion, it hits me how much has gone down these last few months. This place, once intimidating, now feels like a joke. Making my way to the kitchen, I am lost in thought, reflecting on the wild tapestry of fear, bravery, and unexpected affection that has threaded itself through my life. The idea of grabbing an early breakfast with my mom gives me a boost of motivation.

With every step I take, the aroma of fresh coffee and the gentle buzz of morning preparations meet me as my mom gets set for her day. "Morning, Mom," I greet her. "Good morning, sunshine." I smile at her, take a mug, and pour some coffee into it. "Damn, what's the matter with you smiling at me like that?" Valentina's voice makes me laugh softly as I bring the cup to my lips to blow in. "Nothing. I hope you will have a nice girl's day today. And I'm honest. I don't know when we'll eat again together."

She smiles at me and sits down at a small bistro table directly in the kitchen. She peels an orange and forms a smiling little man on the plate with the pieces. It makes me laugh, and I walk over to sit with her. "You used to do that to me a lot when I was little." She smiled. "I know. You loved that a lot." Something new is painted on her face, regret perhaps. She puts a hand on mine. "I'm sorry, Fallon. I didn't protect you properly when you were little. But I always tried to make sure that you had whatever you wanted in life." I feel bad for her. Looking at her face, I see a woman who was abused a lot in her life. Probably more than me. And I know that, in a certain way, she has endured a lot for me. Despite the neglect, despite her absences.

After a quick lunch of fruit and pastry, I decided it was time to go. I received a message earlier from Cam. He had just woken up and was looking for me. After I told him I was with my mother, he told me to take the time I needed with her and come and join him at the cache afterward.

I stand up and place a light kiss on Valentina's head. She freezes and doesn't move. The silence between the two of us is not awkward. Rather, it's a time when we enjoy each other's presence.

My stomach knots as I step into the garage. Daniel looks at me, and I ask him to drive me, his normally carefree demeanor replaced by a face of concern. "I don't like this, not one bit," he confesses, hands gripping the steering wheel with white-knuckled intensity. His worry is a tangible thing, thick in the air between us. I want to reassure him, to say that everything will be fine, but the truth is, I'm not sure of anything anymore. Instead, I offer a half-hearted smile, which does little to ease the tension. "If something happens to you or Camden, I don't know how I will control myself." Arriving at the shop, I find Camden already absorbed in preparations. He's super focused, taking his time cleaning his gun and double-checking our stuff. Without a sound, I ease into the space behind him, my arms reaching out to wrap around his torso. His body heat seeps through his shirt, branding my palms with a warmth that spreads through me like wildfire. He's got this strong, steady vibe that just surrounds me. He doesn't jump or anything. Instead, he lets out a deep breath and subtly leans back into my hug. I feel his throat move as he swallows, and with a deliberate tilt of his head, his profile comes into view. Those stormy eyes find mine, a silent conversation sparking between us. His gaze is piercing, hitting me deep inside. Then, gently, I kiss him. That kiss says so much, filled with yearning and emotions. His hands come to rest over mine, his grip firm, reassuring. They travel to a new object, a mask, one that embodies the darkness we both understand too well. It's a skeleton mask, but unlike his, it's a stark black. "This is for you," he murmurs, his voice a low rumble that vibrates through me. "You'll need to hide those golden locks under a hoodie and stay as invisible as you can. Just like I have always done." A shiver traces my spine, not from fear but from the thrill of being his equal. The mask represents more than just anonymity. It's a symbol of the partnership we have forged in shadows and secrets. I nod, sealing the pact with another kiss, this one with a promise of chaos and passion intertwined. As I slip on the mask, feeling the cold touch of the material against my skin, I embrace the role I'm about to play. Camden lays out the plan with surgical precision and a list of do's and don'ts. "Stay with me at all times," he emphasizes, the weight of his gaze heavy upon me. I nod, understanding the gravity of his every word. We're to infiltrate the location, neutralize the threats, and liberate those bound by chains. And waiting in the wings of the Death Valley hospital is a doctor allied with Camden, a piece positioned on the board ready to strike at Camden's signal and kill the other doctors and nurses who don't see the problem with harvesting organs from innocent persons.

As I absorb the details, we're about to embark on a mission that reeks of vengeance and violence, a far cry from any semblance of the life I once knew. Camden's voice is a dark melody as he concludes, "When the time comes, everything burns." His words linger. I feel it then: the rush of adrenaline, the shiver of anticipation, and beneath it all, the undeniable pulse of fear. We're standing on the precipice of a monumental moment, one that will define us in ways I can't yet fathom. After several hours of preparation, revisions, and physical combat training, once again, we are finally dressed and ready. The door creaks open, and we're swallowed by the night.

CHAPTER 37

LOST BUNNY

FALLON

It's the beginning of night, the port a sprawling maze of containers and shadows that stretching like long fingers into the darkness. Camden and I move in silence, our steps synchronized. We slip between pools of light and dark, nearly invisible, two skeleton phantoms on a mission. We position ourselves with a clear view of the harbor, each becoming a sentinel as we survey the area. The heavy scent of saltwater fills the air, mingling with the tang of motor oil. I can hear the distant sounds of the water lapping against the docks, a deceptive lullaby for the lives shattered within these steel confines. Without a word, Camden lifts his weapon. The distributor, a blurry figure in the distance, collapses mid-step, a marionette with its strings cut. The guards, those soulless protectors of a hellish enterprise, follow swiftly, each bullet from Camden's gun a perfect executioner's note that sings through the air. In the chaos of action, my mind fixates on the containers, the helpless people ensnared by this vile trade. The thought of their broken bodies, their fractured dreams, it roils within me, a storm that I cannot and will not ignore. Camden's yells, a low warning, barely register as I break rank, propelled by a force greater than fear, greater than reason. I'm weaving through these containers like I know exactly what I'm doing, ready to strike. My legs hurt with the effort. My gun and knife are in my hands, ready to strike. Guards pop up, lurking in the shadows, but they're no match for the rage within me. Gunshots are muffled whispers and knife thrusts are silent conversations with death. Each fall is a victory, each step forward a march towards liberation. I take down my enemies individually, and my concern for those imprisoned grows stronger. Blood on my face, Cam's voice echoing in the distance; I keep my focus on the sound of the hushed screams echoing off the metal walls, sensing the heaviness of their hopelessness. They haunt me, pushing me deeper into the heart of darkness, where even my own life becomes a negotiable currency for their freedom. With hands that are both steady and trembling, I approach the door of one of the containers, ready to fling it open and flood the darkness with light.

CHAPTER 38

HOSTAGE OF THE HEART

CAMDEN

Chaos erupts everywhere, the night air crackling with gunfire and shouts. Time slows down as I watch Fallon break away, her determined stride toward the container, cutting through the madness. Dropping my gun, I try to follow, but the relentless barrage of bullets anchors me in place. She's too far, and my heart clenches at the sight of her struggle, the sinking realization that I can't reach her in time. "FUCK! " I curse, mind racing, body tensed as the scene unfolds. Desperation crawls under my skin, a furious itch with no relief. I watch helplessly as a guard disarms her, my anger erupting like a volcano long-held dormant, raw, unchecked fucking fury that promises destruction.

My father, that fucking coward, slinks away into a car, his retreat a blur of motion that fuels my rage. I make a split-second decision, leave the mother fucker be for now. Fallon is more important. Gritting my teeth, I start to run, intending to fight my way to her side. I'm not fast enough. I'M NOT FAST ENOUGH! The distance between us stretches with each second. I focus my eyes and see Fallon fall to the ground with a sickening thud, and everything stops. My vision tunnels, red-fringed and sharp, her name a roar torn from my throat. "FALLON!" My hands clench into fists, the urge to annihilate anything between us stronger than ever. I sprint toward her, slicing through the crowd like a blade.

Each fist, each knife that I wield, is an extension of my wrath. Blood sprays, bones crunch, but all I can see is Fallon, motionless. I'm scared to death for her, and that fear's like tunnel vision, pushing me on. With all the gunfire and the danger of getting hit, I really should be scared for myself, too, but heck, that doesn't matter right now. Panic paralyzes me for a moment as I helplessly observe a guard effortlessly strip her of her defenses.

A potent, scorching anger surges through my blood, igniting every ounce of my being, and I feel a feral roar clawing at the edges of my vocal cords. The desperation is a force unto itself. It propels me, driving my actions with an urgency that overrides any sense of caution.

But enemies swarm, too many for me to cut down, and time slips like sand between my fingers. I'm too late. Her name tears from my lips, a rallying cry of desperation and panic. As the hired enforcers spring into action, they scoop up Fallon's unmoving form, hastily loading her into a vehicle like a precious commodity they can't afford to lose. My feet pound the ground as I desperately try to reach her, but to no avail. The truck's engine roars to life, and it takes off, kicking up a thick cloud of dust that coats my throat and blinds my eyes. The feeling of helplessness wraps around me like a shroud as I stand there, engulfed by a swirling tempest of dust mixed with the bitter taste of treachery. The fury within me swells, unstoppable and ferocious, a relentless surge of vengeance that screams for retribution. I'm momentarily disconnected from reality. The world reduced to the hammering of my heart and the sound of my ragged breaths.

But the rage is a guiding force, compelling me forward, and the violence erupts when I lock eyes with the two remaining henchmen. They scarcely have time to register the fury in my gaze before my wrath descends upon them. My hands, instruments of punishment, move with deadly intent, leaving behind nothing but two lifeless forms, silent and still where they've fallen, a testament to the futility of their resistance against my onslaught.

In the midst of this adrenaline-soaked aftermath, it's almost comical how the ordinary vibration of a phone can pierce the haze of violence. A buzz, persistent and jarring against the fabric of my pocket, threatens to anchor me back to a reality I'm not ready to face. With hands that are slick and stained with the indelible evidence of my actions, the crimson lifeblood of my recent foes, I retrieve the phone. What I see on the screen extinguishes the remnants of my fury, replacing it with a cold, sinking dread.

It's a message, simple text on a digital display, yet it carries the weight of a final judgment. The words come from a man who once held the title of father in my life, a title he's since corrupted and voided by his heinous soul.

"Come to the house now if you want to see your bitch one last time." The message sears itself into my mind, a cruel ultimatum that leaves no fucking room for doubt or negotiation. Rage propels me, driving like a madman toward the house. Upon arrival, I'm restrained and handcuffed without giving a fight because I have one goal: save Fallon. A bag over my head, the suffocating darkness, and then nothing until they allow me to see again.

I blink against the dim light, taking in the grisly scene. I'm in what looks like a cave, cages around me, the air heavy with despair. And Fallon, tied to a chair in front of me, bleeding and broken. Franco is there with another man, and they don't hesitate. They torture me, cut into my flesh like I'm nothing but meat. Fallon's cries fill the air, desperate as she struggles against her restraints, trying to reach me. Time is weird. Everything feels in slow motion and fucking fast at the same time. The room is thick with a sinister chill as Franco, flanked by his impassive guards, looms over me. Their eyes like shards of ice, devoid of empathy or warmth. Each deliberate and precise infliction of pain sends shivers down my spine.

The cruel artistry with which they administer each wound strips away fragments of my identity. Fallon's agonized cries pierce the heavy air as she struggles desperately against her restraints. And I can't take it. Her voice, laced with raw terror, resonates in the stark chamber, a heartbreaking soundtrack to my torment. "Leave him! " She cries. My restraints dig into my wrists, my skin chafed raw. It's a relentless, unforgiving pressure that reminds me I'm still alive, but barely. I'm bound, helpless, the shadow of a man I used to be. The pain radiates through me, every heartbeat a laborious task.

No, this is the kind of pain that breaks you, piece by excruciating piece. My consciousness tethered to the raw nerve endings screaming throughout my body. Each slice of the blade sears a line of fire across my skin, drawing crimson artwork that drips in warm trails down my flesh. I can't take it. But I need to, for Fallon. The sharp intakes of my breath contrast with the guard's grunts as he adds another painful mark to my body. I can't hold back the guttural sounds of torment that escape through gritted teeth. His blows are a rhythmic brutality, a pummeling cascade that lands with sickening thuds against my battered form. I need to keep going; while they are on me, they're not on her, and that's what is important.

Each punch strips away layers of resistance, leaving only the bare essence of survival instinct. My world is reduced to darkness and distress, the two dancing a macabre waltz in the confines of my skull. With deliberate slowness, one of the guards planted a small sharp knife into my abdomen. The intimate proximity of his violence is suffocating, and the cries of my little bunny even more painful. He leans close, his breath reeking of malevolence. Fallon's before me, tears streaming down her face as she looks at me. Her eyes are pools of agony, reflecting the torture I've been through, the degradation I've been subjected to. I want to reach out so badly, to comfort her, to erase the fear of etching her beautiful features, but I'm as helpless as a ghost in chains. "Camden," she whispers, her voice cracking. Her form is a blur through the haze of my brain, a trembling mirage that I can't touch, can't protect. The sight of her despair is a dagger twisting in my gut, the one thing I can't bear to witness, even though the shroud of my own torment. She bites her lip, trying to stifle the sobs that threaten to claw their way out. I wish I could tell her it'll be all right, that I've got a plan, but the words are a gallows-hung lie. All I can do is stare back at her, my gaze burning with unspoken apologies and a ferocity that hasn't been extinguished, not yet. My body may be shackled, but my will. That's something they can't tie down. The dank air clings to me, a cold shroud that smells of rust and dread. Every breath I take is laced with the metal tang of blood and the simmering threat of death. "Don't cry for me, baby," I rasp, my voice a hoarse whisper that's barely audible over the echoes of our nightmare. "This isn't the end, not for us. " But even as I say it, I can feel the grip of darkness tightening, the encroaching void that promises nothing but oblivion. My mind is a battlefield, waging war between the urge to submit to the darkness and the burning need to fight back, to rise. I see it in her eyes, the fierce determination that mirrors my own. Even as her tears carve silent paths down her cheeks, there's a strength that refuses to be quelled. She's a warrior, my warrior, and I know she won't give up on me. A man pushed to the edge of his limits is a dangerous thing, but a woman... fucking terrifying. After seconds that seem to stretch to eternity, the man leaves me alone and steps back. Franco appears in the middle and looks at me with a smile before turning to Fallon. "Little Fallon, so fragile, so full of life, gasping for breath under the oppressive weight of illness. Oh, those naive years when her little lungs struggled to draw air, a pitiful fight against the inevitable demise. Your mom was super sad, you know, just hanging on to what little was left of you. It was kind of sad to see. Getting your hands on something as pricey as a new lung is like hitting the jackpot, a dream too big for her bank account. So, she did what she had to, using the only thing she could offer up: herself. Yeah, a rich dude's fun time in exchange for her kid's life. Pretty rough trade, huh? But when you're backed into a corner, you don't really play by the rules, do you? And when things were at their worst, who did she call? I, Franco Betto, am the hotshot of the not-so-legal organ business. It was an opportunity to save your life and see how far I could push my empire. Just making money the legit way wasn't enough for me. I wanted more, always more. You, Fallon, you were my test run, the first one to get a 'special delivery' from my stash, a lung that gave you a second shot at life. But that kind of present doesn't come without a cost. But I needed a test donor, too; what a perfect coincidence I had a kid, useless, should I add. He didn't have a say in it, but he was key to the whole thing. But that's just how it goes. Life's tough, and I'm just playing my part. Messed up how I linked you and Camden together after all these years, huh? Tying your lives together with the very thing that keeps you breathing. You're alive 'cause Camden had to give up a piece of himself, and now, with every breath you take, you're reminded of that connection. It's like some twisted poetry, right? Now, here you both are, like a hurricane and a wildfire, taking on the world. But don't forget, Fallon, every single breath, every heartbeat that keeps you going, it's all thanks to me." Completely shocked and on the verge of passing out, I lock eyes with Franco, who's now facing me again.

"Hey Camden, my kid who's gone off the path, isn't life weird? You're stuck to her like glue, all because of blood and breath. She's gonna be your downfall. Man, When I reconnected with Valentina, I wasn't interested, but then I remembered little Fallon, taught, why not make her my new property, my daughter since she owns me anyway. Didn't think you sack of shit would make her fall in love with you." This connection, made through Franco's terrible actions, links Fallon and me in a very close and wrong way. Our lives and bodies have been joined because of the choices of a man who only sees us as things to use in his horrible business.

When I wrote that scene, I was listening to music, and that's the song that started. I thought it was perfect. Listen to it to get into the mood.

Infinity- Jaymes Young

CHAPTER 40

WOMEN STRENGTH

FALLON

Shock pulses through me, a deafening rush that eclipses all rational thought as I witness the vital essence draining from Camden's form. My heart fractures, a myriad of jagged pieces strewn by the harsh winds of this brutal truth. Rage, a tempest of fiery, untamed emotion, surges through my veins. *I'll kill them all.* The revelation hits me like a fucking tsunami wave, choking my very breath from myself, and a sense of betrayal burns deep into my very being, searing through to the core of my soul.

The knowledge that his own father could inflict this upon him, a person who has become an integral part of my life, ignites an inferno of fury inside me, howling for retribution and justice for the wrongs committed. The intensity of my emotions is overwhelming. I'll *kill them all.*

The world feels like it suddenly shifts when Daniel and Valentina break the quietness of the room. They enter quickly and with a burst, bringing the chaos of a fight with the guards. As bullets fly through the silence, they make a definite impact on the thick tension in the air. Daniel moves through the confusion like he knows exactly what he's doing, shooting his gun in quick bursts. Each shot he fires quickly takes down a guard, who falls to the ground. *I'll kill them all.*

Valentina fights with a fierce energy, right there with him, her anger showing in every move. Her gun fires rapidly, hitting her targets with deadly precision. Together, they create a surprising performance, the strong smell of gunpowder mixing with the metallic scent of blood.

As Franco's anger grows really strong, the tension in the room is thick and heavy. He lifts his gun, his hand not shaking at all, and points it at Daniel. I try to scream, to let him know, and we look at each other deeply; Daniel's eyes send me a silent message of farewell before he falls to the ground, no longer alive, a victim too. *I'll kill them all.*

I'm filled with rage, rage, fucking rage, and my loud crying echoes around the room, turning into a sad song that tells our story. As I'm yelling, Valentina comes to me; she quickly tries to free me, her tears falling too as she tells me that Daniel had trusted her and told her what was going on, that she wanted to protect me, give me a good life, that she will always love me. Our tears mix together, becoming a sign of our combined sadness and the love between a mother and her child. The room is still filled with the sound of my crying, and Franco's mean voice breaks the quiet. "Dirty whore!" With a terrible calmness, he fires the gun, and he doesn't miss Valentina's head. In just a moment, she's no longer warm. Her body falls limp in my arms. *I'll kill them all.*

A scream comes out of me, so loud and full of hurt that it seems to fucking wake up hell itself. Our connection is cut off so quickly and violently, leaving me alone with my grief, reaching out for the love that's not there anymore. The echoes of gunshots have faded, but their impact reverberates through my body as I stand in shocked silence. Franco has vanished, his absence as glaring as the stark splashes of blood painting the floor a violent shade of red. *I'll kill them all.*

I run to Camden, his once strong and defiant presence now frighteningly fragile in my arms. His life force is ebbing away, each second another precious heartbeat fading, like the relentless ticking of an ancient clock counting down our moments together.

Dragging him with all the strength I can muster, I wrap my fingers around his wrists, the weight of his body heavy for my tired body. Adrenaline becomes my ally, igniting within me a spark of unexpected power. My emotions transform into raw physical force. I'm fueled by a mixture of fury and heart-wrenching sorrow as I pull him, inch by agonizing inch, toward the promise of an escape. *I'll kill them all.*

Once outside the looming shadow of the building, my legs give way, and I crumble to the ground, Camden's limp form beside me. Heaving breaths escape my lips, my chest rising and falling in frantic rhythm as I clutch the gun next to me, the cold metal a grim reminder of our reality. With each plea that escapes my lips for him to cling to life, my voice shatters further, splintering under the weight of terror and urgency.

Somehow, despite my trembling hands and the biting cold that seemed to seek out the marrow of my bones, I found the resolve to continue. I heave Camden's body into his car, every move I make haunted by the specter of dread that clings to me like a second skin. *I'll kill them all.*

I speed through the city and the desolate roads to Death Valley. The inky sky above us seems to press down with an unbearable weight, the stars too distant to offer any semblance of hope. I drive with one hand on the wheel and the other clutching Camden's arms, seeking reassurance in the faint pulse beneath his skin. The journey to the trusted surgeon feels like an eternity, each mile stretching out before us, filled with the tension of a life hanging in the balance. Every moment is a battle against time.

My tears are relentless, a torrent of grief that no dam could hold back. They cascade down my cheeks, each one a liquid testament to the depth of my fear for Camden. I whisper silent bargains to any deity listening, each tear a wordless entreaty for his survival. The sound of my breaths is frantic, harsh against the silence that ensues as I push the car to its limits. Camden's car. The speedometer needle climbs a race against time, my hands gripping the wheel with white-knuckled desperation. I'm a tempest behind the wheel. Fallon, drive fucking faster.

I flinch as Camden's groan slices through my concentration. Every cell in my body screams to keep him alive. The hospital lights loom in the distance, a beacon amidst my storm of panic. I can't let him die. I refuse. *I'll kill them all.*

We arrive at the hospital, the air thick with the tang of blood. Camden, his body a map of torture and red, is teetering on the brink of consciousness. As the car screeches to a halt in front of the doors, I'm already reaching for Camden, clutching his hand, a lifeline that anchors us together. "Hold on, please," I choke out between sobs, my vision blurred as I stagger out of the car, half-dragging, half-carrying him into the glaring brightness of the entrance. "Please, Camden, don't leave me."

I'm a mess of memories and fears as they wheel him away; the doctor on our side comes rushing, swarming him like a force of nature, his hands confident where mine tremble. Daniel's gone, my mother's gone, and now Camden's fighting for each breath. *I'll kill them all.*

I bury my face in my hands, the metallic scent of Camden's blood strong on my skin. Images flash before my eyes: his smile, the softness I've glimpsed in his eyes when he looks at me, the curve of his tattooed chest that has held me close in the night. Fallon, stay strong. You can do this.

I recall the strength in his grip, the fierce protectiveness in his every action. His words, dark and promising, reverberate in my mind, "Trust no one." But right now, trust is all I have left: trust in the doctors and trust in the love that binds our twisted souls.

As I gaze down the empty corridor, it's his love that fills the hollow spaces of my heart, his love that's a fire in my veins. *I'll kill them all.* With the desert winds as our solemn witness, I vow to protect Camden with every fiber of my being. I will fight against the encroaching shadows, against the cruel hands of fate that dare to snatch him away from this world, from me.

His hand, a pale contrast to the bruises that mar his skin, trembles as it ascends through the air, a silent rebel against his body's failing. His fingers brush my cheek, a whisper of contact. I close my eyes to the contact. With all his power, all his will, he locks eyes with me and murmurs.

"I love you."

To be continued...

ABOUT THE AUTHOR

Step into the world of Maryse Marullo, that explore the haunting beauty of love in the shadows. Hailing from the landscapes of Canada. Maryse is an author who thrives on the edges of passion and darkness, crafting narratives that delve into the depths of the human heart. She's addicted to dark, taboo, and forbidden romance.

Follow her on TikTok and Instagram for updates on upcoming releases and a glimpse into the mind behind the captivating tales of dark romance.

https://beacons.ai/authormarysemarullo

As you finish the pages of this book, I hope you find it both captivating and thought-provoking. However, I recognize that real-life situations can be challenging. If you, or someone you know, is facing a dangerous situation or is in need of assistance, I strongly encourage you to take action.

Your safety and well-being are of utmost importance to me. Do not hesitate to reach out to local authorities, emergency services, or a specialized hotline. You are not alone, and there are people ready to help.

Do not ignore warning signs. Together, we can contribute to creating a safer environment for everyone.

Take care of yourself, be attentive to those around you, and don't hesitate to seek help if needed.

Maryse xxx

www.ingramcontent.com/pod-product-compliance
Lightning Source LLC
Chambersburg PA
CBHW021235190726
48289CB00005B/1327